PRAISE FOR SANDRA BROWN

"Romance fans will want to curl up with this one."
—*Boston Herald*

"A very fast-paced, quick read. Delightful."
—*Philadelphia Inquirer*

"Read with a hanky close by." —*Tampa Tribune*

"A novelist who can't write fast enough."
—*San Antonio Express-News*

"Author Sandra Brown proves herself top-notch."
—Associated Press

"Nobody in the '90s has had more hits. . . . Brown's storytelling gift [is] surprisingly rare, even among crowd-pleasers." —*Toronto Sun*

"She knows how to keep the tension high and the plot twisting and turning." —*Fresno Bee*

Heaven's Price

Price

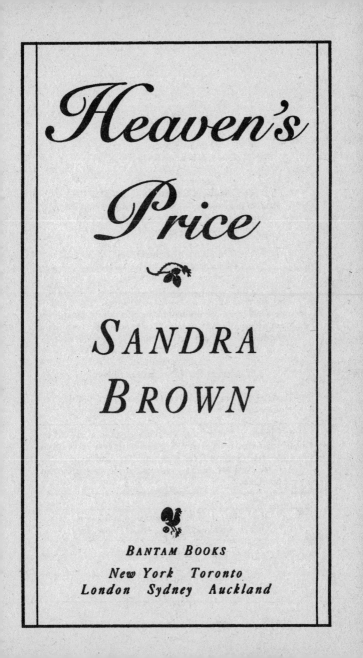

SANDRA
BROWN

BANTAM BOOKS

New York   Toronto
London   Sydney   Auckland

HEAVEN'S PRICE
A Bantam Book

PUBLISHING HISTORY
Bantam Loveswept edition published May 1983
Bantam hardcover edition published January 1995
Bantam paperback edition / December 1995
Bantam mass market reissue / May 2007

Published by Bantam Dell
A Division of Random House, Inc.
New York, New York

Library of Congress Catalog Card Number: 94-20158

Bantam Books and the rooster colophon are
registered trademarks of Random House, Inc.

ISBN 978-0-553-59017-3

Printed in the United States of America

www.bantamdell.com

OPM 10 9 8 7 6 5 4 3 2 1

Dear Reader,

You have my wholehearted thanks for the interest and enthusiasm you've shown for my Loveswept romances over the past decade. I'm enormously pleased that the enjoyment I derived from writing them was contagious. Obviously you share my fondness for love stories that always end happily and leave us with a warm inner glow.

Nothing quite equals the excitement one experiences when falling in love. In each romance, I tried to capture that excitement. The settings and characters and plots changed, but that was the recurring theme.

Something in all of us delights in lovers and their uneven pursuit of mutual fulfillment and happiness. Indeed, the pursuit is half the fun! I became deeply involved with each pair of lovers and their unique story. As though paying a visit to old friends for whom I played matchmaker, I often reread their stories myself.

I hope you enjoy this encore edition of one of my personal favorites.

SANDRA BROWN

Chapter 1

Blair carted the last box up the top three stairs. Squeezing herself between it and the jamb, she maneuvered it through the door and dropped it down on top of two others piled just inside the door. Her arms quivered from the exertion. Her legs ached.

"Thank heaven that's the last one," she said to herself on an exhalation that escaped her lips slowly and leisurely. With rigid arms she braced herself over the top of the box and tried to catch her breath. When she straightened, she noticed the tightness of the muscles in her lower back and groaned. Was there any part of her body that didn't ache?

Glancing down at her wristwatch, her lips thinned

with irritation. She had called the YMCA over two hours ago and asked them to send over a masseur. Not having changed residences in more than eight years, she had forgotten how physically exhausting moving could be. A massage was the most relaxing thing she could think of. Since her telephone hadn't been installed yet, she had driven to the nearest service station and used the pay phone. The receptionist who answered the Y's telephone had assured her that someone would be sent over within an hour.

"So much for efficiency," she muttered to herself, whisking off the bandana-print scarf she had tied around her long dark hair. It tumbled to the middle of her back like a bolt of satin being unrolled. If the staff of the YMCA typified the pace of life in this provincial backwater town, she'd be a raving maniac in a week.

She gazed around the three-room apartment that would be her home for the next six months. It didn't look like much now with boxes and bundles heaped on its hardwood floors, but with a little imagination, she hoped she could make it at least livable. Pam had assured her that it was the best and most private place in town, ". . . unless you want to live in one of those sterile apartment complexes, which I'm sure you don't," she had added.

Upon arrival from the city to the small town on the Atlantic side of Long Island where her friend Pam Delgado had moved several years ago, Blair had to admit that living in a garage apartment behind a

Victorian house on a quiet, tree-shaded street had more appeal than living in a concrete cracker box.

She skirted the maze of boxes as she made her way to the small kitchen on the other side of the large room that served as both living and sleeping area. She had been pleased to see that the refrigerator was no more than two decades old and had a bucket inside the freezing compartment in which to empty ice trays. Taking out a few cubes, she plunked them into a tall glass she'd managed to find earlier and popped off the top of a diet soda can. Just as it was foaming over the ice, someone knocked on the door.

"Wouldn't you know it," she grumbled. Taking a sip of the not yet cold drink, she weaved her way through the boxes again and pulled open the door.

"It's about time," she said querulously.

"I beg your pardon," the man on the doorstep said.

Blair's green eyes were level with a massive chest and she had to lift them a considerable distance to greet the most intriguing pair of eyes she'd ever encountered. Startlingly blue, they were surrounded by thick, curling lashes, dark at the lashline and gilded at the tips. A network of weblike lines, white against darkly tanned skin, extended from the outer corners of his eyes to fade into his temples. Brows well defined, but thick, arched over the eyes that were examining her as closely as she was him.

To avoid that careful scrutiny, she quickly lowered her eyes, mistakenly thinking that would be the safest thing to do. She wasn't prepared for them com-

ing to rest on a golden-brown mustache, the exact
color of the brows that framed his eyes. The mustache curved over a wide, sensuous mouth. Beneath
sculptured lips was a strong, firm chin with a vertical
dent carved into its center. She avoided analyzing
that too, and lifted her eyes to take in a well-designed
nose, slightly concave cheeks, and assertive cheek-
bones, which brought her back to those eyes. They
hadn't wavered from her face.

All in all, it was the most marvelous assembly of
masculine features Blair had ever seen. She felt like
stammering, but somehow managed not to when she
demanded, "Didn't anyone tell you how to get
here?"

He shook the head that was capped with blond
wavy hair, slightly silvered at the temples. "No."

"Well, it's no wonder you're over an hour late.
None of the streets in this town are marked with
signs," she said crossly. Stepping aside, she said,
"Come on in. I need you more now than I did when I
called."

He stepped through the door and she closed it
behind him to conserve the air that flowed from the
one-window air-conditioning unit that cooled the entire apartment. He hadn't brought any equipment in
with him, only a body that would intimidate the most
fearsome professional football lineman.

Clad in white shorts and a navy-blue T-shirt, the
man looked marvelous. Blair could see that the tan
that bronzed his face covered the rest of him, as did
that fine curly golden hair. His legs were long and

lean, but muscles rippled in his calves and thighs as he made slow progress around the first boxes blocking his path. Blair excused her interest in those muscles as purely professional. She was well acquainted with every muscle of the human body, its use, and how to treat it.

"Didn't you bring a portable bed or table or anything with you?" she asked.

He stopped suddenly and turned around to face her. "No."

She sighed. "It's just as well. I don't know where we would have put it. I've already padded the kitchen table with a quilt. Will that be all right?" He turned his head to eye the table dubiously. "I haven't made up the bed in the sofa yet and didn't want to plow through all these boxes looking for linens. I need you right now. Do you mind doing it on the kitchen table?"

His eyes crinkled at the corners, but there wasn't even the slightest smiling twitch of his mustache when he answered levelly, "Not at all."

His laconic answers annoyed her. She felt like a babbling moron while he remained aloof, watching her with indulgent amusement. He hadn't even apologized for being late. But then he didn't look like a man to whom apologies would come easily. He was looking at her steadily with a curiosity he couldn't disguise. She strongly suspected that lying just beneath his placid features was a booming laugh dying to be freed. Why, she couldn't fathom.

She tracked the path his eyes took down the

length of her petite body. Never having known a moment's modesty in her life, the sudden impulse to cover herself was foreign, but there nonetheless. His eyes seemed to wash over her, leaving behind a blushing stain everywhere they touched. There was certainly nothing alluring in her attire, yet his slow, silent appraisal made her feel that the denim cutoffs and white eyelet halter-top were the flimsiest of negligees.

Had he made some lascivious remark like the ones that were often thrown to her on the streets of New York, she would have flung back a scathing insult. Or had he commented clinically on her good muscle tone, the length and formation of her legs, her graceful carriage, she would have thanked him and never given it a thought. Those kinds of comments she could handle. The ones eloquently transmitted by his eyes, she had no comebacks for.

"Well, shall we get started?" The corners of his mouth lifted in the suggestion of a smile.

His voice sent a shiver up her spine. It seemed to caress her ears with its deep rumbling timbre. How else could it sound since it originated in that chest? "Don't you want me to undress first?"

One brow leaped into a quizzical arch over his eye. "I guess so. Yes."

"I'll be just a minute then." She hurried into the bathroom, where earlier she had brought out an old sheet from one of the boxes. Her fingers fumbled with the fastening on her shorts. What was wrong with her? Why was she so nervous? She'd had massages before, many in the privacy of her apartment in Manhattan. Never had she been anxious about it. She hadn't been anxious about this one until she'd seen the masseur. Maybe if the guy bothered her so much, she shouldn't go through with it.

One shooting pain from her legs told her she would be foolhardy to pass up this opportunity. Her abused muscles needed soothing, and the doctor had recommended this sort of therapy. She was being silly. In her nearly thirty years, she'd never been fainthearted about anything. Wrapping the sheet around her naked body, she boldly opened the bathroom door and stepped out.

"I take it you didn't bring any lotion either," she said, brushing past him disdainfully.

"No, I didn't bring any lotion."

"I should be glad. Sometimes the lotions masseurs use smell medicinal. You can use this." She handed him the plastic bottle of lotion she'd brought from the bathroom. It was scented with her favorite fragrance. "And here are some towels for when you . . . for when you need them," she finished self-consciously, extending him the folded terrycloth towels.

She wished he wouldn't look at her as though he were about to devour her. She had shared matchbox-sized dressing rooms with men and women all racing to get into the next costume change. Often she'd been forced to forgo a trip to the dressing room and change just offstage with no screening whatsoever.

Why now was she seized by a maidenly awareness of her nakedness beneath the sheet?

In hopes of distracting him from his absorption with her bare shoulders, she said, "I . . . I was drinking a soda when you arrived. Would you care for one?"

"No thank you. Maybe when we're done."

She looked away from him and moved to the rectangular table in the kitchen that was barely long enough for her to lie on. She had draped it with an old quilt she'd found in the top of one of the apartment's two closets.

"That looks comfortable," he said.

"The table?"

"The quilt."

"Oh," she looked down at the faded spread. "I guess so. It isn't mine. It came with the apartment."

"I take it you're just moving in."

"Yes."

She turned her back to him and lay face down on the table, stretching out and adjusting herself as comfortably as she could. The quilt didn't do much in the way of padding the hard surface. Raising herself up, she unfolded the sheet and spread it out on either side of her until her front was lying directly on the laundered-soft quilt. Folding her hands one on top of the other, she lay her cheek on the back of the top one and turned her face away from him.

"Do you like the apartment?"

"It's okay for someplace temporary. I'll be here six months at the most."

"Are you from the city?"

"Not originally," she answered. She held her breath for a moment when she felt him raise the sheet and slide a towel over her hips, covering them.

"Originally where are you from?"

"Minnesota." The word came out in a gush of air as his palm held the towel over her hips in place while he tossed the sheet aside. Naked but for the towel, which felt about as large as a Band-Aid across her derriere, she could all but feel his scorching blue eyes as they surveyed the expanse of bare skin.

Long moments passed. He didn't speak. She didn't breathe. Neither moved. Finally, unable to bear the suspense, she turned her head toward him. "Is something wrong?"

He cleared his throat. "No. Nothing. I was just flexing my fingers."

"Oh."

She felt rather than saw his movements as he poured some lotion onto his palm and spread it to the other one by rubbing his hands together. Then his hands settled on her shoulders. Moving slowly at first, he bore down gently on the tense muscles and smoothed the scented lotion over them. Increasing the pressure slightly, his hands began to work a magic and Blair felt her tension dissolving.

"Have you worked for the Y long?"

"The Y?"

"Yes, have you worked there long?"

"Uh . . . no. Actually I don't work there. I sort of free-lance."

"I see. Do you have enough clients to keep you busy in a town this size?"

"You'd be surprised."

Both hands were on one shoulder now, squeezing the ever-relaxing muscles. "Your hands don't feel like most masseurs'. They have calluses."

"I'm sorry."

"I wasn't complaining. It was only an observation."

"I work out with weights fairly often. They leave calluses."

"So you're into all kinds of physical fitness."

"I guess you could say that."

"I thought so. You seem very fit."

"So do you." He chose that moment to slide his hands from her shoulders to just beneath her raised arms where his fingers curved into the tender, sensitive skin. The heels of his hands were planted in the groove of her spine and Blair realized how large and strong they were. With only the merest pressure, they could crack her ribs. She breathed easier when they began a gradual descent and his fingers were no longer touching that particular spot underneath her arms.

"I'm a dancer. I have to stay in shape."

"What kind of dancer? A ballerina?"

"I attend ballet class every day to work out, but I dance mostly in musical comedies."

"Hey! What shows have you been in?"

She laughed lightly. "At one time or another

nearly all of them, both on and off Broadway. Sometimes with a road company for months at a time."

"You've been at it for a long time then."

"Yes. Since graduating from high school. Much to my parents' dismay, I came to New York when everyone else was going off to state college."

"They didn't want you to?"

"That's an understatement. Even getting my degree by going to night classes didn't convince them that I wasn't on the road to destruction. I had told them for years that I was going to New York to study and dance and they humored me, thinking I'd outgrow the notion, or that I'd meet some nice hometown boy and replace hopeless dreams with marriage."

"But you didn't."

"No."

"Surely they're proud of you now."

"Yes, but it's a qualified pride," she replied slowly. Reminders of the heartache she had brought her parents always made her sad. For so many years she had sought their approval of her way of life. It was an impossible dream that she would never attain, for they would never understand her compulsion to dance. "They won't consider me successful until I marry and present them with a passel of grandchildren."

His thumbs were melting each vertebra with a revolving, mesmerizing motion. When they met at the base of her spine, his palms settled over the top curve of her hips. The towel slipped a few inches. Without sacrificing pressure, his hands massaged, taking skin, muscles, and weariness with them. Blair's eyes closed with a sigh of pure physical pleasure.

"You must be their one and only."

"That's just it," she mumbled sleepily against the back of her hand, "I have two brothers and a sister who have provided them with more grandchildren than they can afford to keep in birthday presents."

He chuckled and she liked the sound. It was as soothing as his hands, which were raising her hips slightly with each gentle squeeze only to press them back onto the soft quilt with the next downward stroke. "I guess that's the way parents are. They're not happy until their children conform to their idea of success."

"Maybe there's hope for the next generation of parents. My friend Pam has five children and she treats each one as an individual. You may know her. She lives here in Tidelands and is responsible for my being here. Pam Delgado."

"I know the Delgados. He's a policeman, isn't he?"

"Yes." Blair laughed, barely noticing that his hands were once again spanning her ribs. "If you'd known Pam ten years ago, you'd never believe her now. She gave up dance to marry Joe and live in the suburbs. I still can't quite believe that my friend who suffered through starvation diets and rigorous classes with me is now the happy mother of five little Delgados."

"You don't approve of her decision?"

Blair shrugged her shoulders. "It wasn't for me to approve or disapprove. It's just that I can't understand anyone giving up dance who isn't absolutely forced."

His fingers were trailing up and down her sides over her ribs while the heels of his hands made lazy progress up her spine. Blair was jolted to the soles of her feet when his fingers brushed the sides of her breasts, plumped out against the quilt. She shifted her weight and he got the less-than-subtle message. His hands left her long enough to get more lotion. When next he began, they were on the backs of her knees.

"If you're so dedicated to dance, what are you doing here? It doesn't seem convenient to move out here to Long Island when you've lived in the city for so many years."

He was kneading the muscles of one calf with both hands. The rhythmic motion brought on a delicious lassitude and Blair relaxed again. She didn't want to admit, even to herself, how it had alarmed her when she'd felt the feathery touch of his fingers at the sides of her breasts. Her heart had thudded against the hard surface of the table and the blood in her veins had seemed to concentrate in her earlobes, making them throb. Now that his movements had returned to those of the detached masseur, she could only think that what had happened had been an accident or that she had been unaccountably touchy.

After all, every part of her body had been handled by men for years. When one danced with a partner, the execution of a step often depended on the hold. Such holds left no room for timidity or modesty. But though she had been handled with much more intimacy, she didn't recall when a touch had made her throat constrict or when it had made her stomach feel like it would sink to the top of her thighs only to explode in a shower of tickling sensations.

"Did I miss your answer?"

The sound of his voice as he leaned close to her ear roused her from the momentary lethargy. Even though she could have done without his breath fanning her ear, she was glad he had pulled her from her musings that were becoming increasingly disturbing. She stirred restlessly as his hands moved up to the backs of her thighs. "I'm sorry. I . . . I have to stop dancing for awhile under doctor's orders."

Both hands stroking her thighs came to a standstill. "Why?"

"My knees mostly. I have some tendon and cartilage damage that needs time to knit."

"How long before you can dance again?"

"Six months," she said quietly, remembering again the anguish that had pierced through her when she heard the doctor say those fatal words. He was the third specialist she had consulted, not accepting the diagnoses of the first two, but passing them off as charlatans who didn't give as much thought to her knees as they did her checkbook.

The hands began massaging again. "That sounds serious."

"Well it's not," she snapped. She closed her eyes,

squeezing out the facts she didn't want to accept. "It's not," she said more softly, but with just as much conviction. "Things like this happen to professional dancers all the time—tendinitis, muscle sprain, shin splints. A few months' rest and I'll be fine."

"You can't dance at all?"

"I can do minimal workouts to retain muscle tone. Nothing strenuous."

They were quiet for a moment as she tried to block two things from her consciousness. First, the agony of having to give up her career for even six months. Second, the riotous sensations plaguing the erogenous parts of her body with each touch of his callused fingers on the backs of her thighs.

"Did you carry all those boxes up by yourself?" he asked at last, breaking the heavy silence.

"Yes. Pam lent me her station wagon for a few days. I drove it from the city this morning and didn't want to wait for anyone to help me unload it."

"Carrying all that weight up the stairs couldn't have been good for your knees."

"It didn't hurt them." Actually they had been hurting by the time the last of the boxes had been carried to the second story, but she wanted to deny that just as she wanted to deny that there was anything wrong with them in the first place. She was playing a childish game with herself and she knew it. Ignoring the problem wouldn't make it go away. But she wasn't ready to admit that she might have to give up dancing forever. That was as good as admitting that she would have to give up breathing, for to her one was as essential to life as the other.

"Surely you could have asked for someone to help you."

"Pam's children had planned to go to the beach today and I told her not to disappoint them. She said she and Joe would come over later to help me, but I didn't want to wait that late, much less impose on them. There's a man who lives in the house across from me. I'm leasing the apartment from him. Pam said to ask him for anything I needed, but I haven't seen him. He had given Pam a key for me and I picked it up from her this morning."

"You haven't met him then?"

"No, he's a friend of Pam's and she handled the leasing for me. He's a carpenter or something like that."

"I'm sure he wouldn't have minded helping a dainty thing like you lug all those boxes up here."

"Probably not," Blair said, dismissing the possibility, "but I don't want to be obligated to my neighbors."

"I see. You're independent."

"Totally. And I like it that way."

She heard a chair scrape across the floor as he pulled it to the end of the table. A glance over her shoulder showed him sitting down. She felt uncannily relieved that he was no longer touching her thighs.

Taking one of her slender feet in his palm, he began stroking the sole with his thumb. "What in the world did you do to these feet?"

She laughed. "Ugly, aren't they? Toe shoes, blisters worn into calluses, bigger blisters, more calluses—after years of dancing, a dancer's feet look like hooves."

He laved lotion over the bumps and knobs. She wouldn't have let him smooth them away if she were going to be dancing. It took a while to build up calluses hard enough to withstand the brutality heaped on them. Instead she gave in to the luxury of having his fingers stroke and press. Each of her toes was squeezed through a wringer made by his strong fingers.

He lifted her feet one at a time and rotated the ankle. "No, no, relax," he said quietly when she began to do his work for him. "Let me move it." When he was finished with her feet, he stood and bent her knee back, rotating it in the same way, but gently enough not to hurt her. She relinquished what small control she stubbornly maintained and let him work the kinks out of the tired muscles until her joints seemed to move as they hadn't for weeks.

After giving the second leg the same treatment, he lay it back down on the quilt. A weighty languor blanketed her until she felt like every bone in her body had gone as limp as a noodle. Her eyelids refused to remain open. She never wanted this hour with the man with the gifted hands to end. He had given her the relaxation she'd thought she'd never know again after leaving the doctor's plush Park Avenue office and limping home with tears of angry frustration rolling down her cheeks.

"You can turn over now," a low, compelling voice instructed her. She gave no thought to disobeying, but rolled over with one supple motion, her eyes still closed. She heard what could have been a soft gasp of surprise before she felt the cool towels being spread across her breasts and lower abdomen. Something about that gasp should have bothered her, she knew, but was too sleepy to concentrate on it.

He moved to the other end of the table to stand behind her head. She knew he was pouring more lotion into his palm by the heady fragrance that suffused her nostrils. When he leaned forward to return the bottle to the table, she felt the pressure of his thighs against the top of her head. She heard the lotion squishing in his hands before he lay them gently on the front of her shoulders. With long, measured strokes, he smoothed the emulsion along her upper arms. His breath fell like a mist on her face.

His fingers curved around her shoulders while his thumbs explored her collarbone. His touch was light, tentative, and unnecessary to a therapeutic massage, but Blair didn't see any value in pointing that out. It was too sublime to lie beneath those marvelous hands and wonder what whimsical mood would strike them next.

Her idle curiosity was soon satisfied, as his hands slowly descended to graze the upper portion of her chest. Her skin experienced a rebirth beneath his touch. A seed of desire burst open deep inside her breasts and blossomed outward until her nipples tautened with awakening. She yearned to be caressed by the hands that could bring about such wonders. Had she not been so drugged by his fingers drifting ever closer to what begged to be touched, she would have taken his hands under her own and dragged them down, pressing them to her aching breasts and swollen nipples. When his hands reluctantly withdrew to safer terrain, she didn't identify that strange garbled sound as her own whimpering protest.

He lifted one of her lifeless arms by the hand and, stretching it up to its full length, rested it against his chest. Applying minimal pressure, he squeezed the fragile muscles. His fingers could encircle each part of her arm as they inched upward from her armpit to her hand that lay like a wilted flower against his massive chest. Her fingertips knew the airy caress of his breath as he bowed his head to observe his effectiveness.

Blair wondered what he would do should she reach up to touch the cleft in his chin or drag her index finger across the brush of his mustache. She lacked the energy to carry out such a notion even if she had had the temerity, which she didn't. But thinking about it made her insides feel warm and heavy, as though a thick, sweet syrup were flowing through her veins.

The fingers of the massaging hand finally reached her wrist. They gripped it lightly while the thumb of the other hand impressed concentric circles into her palm. He rocked her hand back and forth on the pivotal bones of her wrist, persuading her to surrender all control to him. Methodically he massaged each of her fingers, beginning at the base and working his way up to the tip. The fleshy pad of each finger was caressed by the corresponding part of his thumb. It might well have been his tongue for the thorough, thrusting, darting, erotic seduction it performed on each fingertip.

Blair, with what mental capacity she had left, ordered her eyes to open and make sure that such was not the case. Her eyes slammed into the stunning blue ones that were staring down at her. He lifted her other arm and lay it against his chest like its partner. He secured them there by moving his arms in front of them and placing his elbows in the undersides of hers.

"Have I ever seen you dance?" he asked in the tone of a hypnotist asking, "Are you asleep now?" His hands closed around her jaw, his thumbs massaging just in front of her ears.

Grateful she still had the wherewithal to understand her native language she said gruffly, "I don't know. Have you?"

"Tell me something I might have seen you in."

Her eyes gave up the fight to remain open when his hands closed around the base of her neck and his thumbs lightly measured its graceful length. "I . . . I was in an orange juice commercial for television," she said breathily.

"Yes?" He was pressing her temples now, rolling her head from side to side. The muscles of his thighs were rock hard against the crown of her head.

"I was a figure on a pinball machine. A giant silver ball rolled toward me and I did a leapfrog over it."

"I've seen that, but—"

"You wouldn't recognize me. I had on a silverfoil wig and huge daisy-shaped sunglasses with bright yellow lenses."

He rested his thumbs at the center of her hairline before following its heart-shaped course around her forehead to her ear. "I can't imagine you in a silver wig. I can't imagine you as having anything but glossy black hair. Daisy-shaped sunglasses with yellow lenses?" he asked softly. "No. Nothing but green eyes as fathomless as the sea." As on command, they opened to give him their full attention. His index finger traced the smooth, perfect arch of her dark brow.

Blair knew she shouldn't be allowing this. He might be a degenerate, a—but she could think of no reason she wanted to stop the inevitable. He trapped her hands against his chest as he bent over her. She could see each facet in his diamond blue eyes and they paralyzed rational thought with their brilliance.

"I can't imagine you as being any way except exactly as you are. I wouldn't change a thing." The fingers that had been caressing her cheeks were replaced by the silky touch of his mustache. Imperceptibly but inexorably he moved closer to her mouth until he hovered above it. She breathed in the intoxicating bouquet of his breath. Just as she was expecting the pressure of his lips on hers, someone knocked on the door.

She stifled her murmur of regret. He sighed and

brought himself upright, releasing her hands and lowering them beside her gently. Hastily she sat up and groped for the sheet, hot color rising to her cheeks as she watched him wade through the boxes to casually open her front door.

"Hi." The voice was masculine, but lacking in maturity. "Sorry to be so late, but someone at the desk got their wires crossed." The tall blond man didn't seem inclined to respond. The younger man, wearing white trousers and a white T-shirt with YMCA printed in red letters on the left breast pocket, said with a questioning inflection, "I'm the masseur."

Chapter 2

The young man's words hit Blair with the impact of a blow from a baseball bat. She sat on the edge of the table, clutching the twisted sheet to her, her hair a tangled dark cloud cloaking her shoulders. Her face, so flushed only moments ago, now drained to a chalky white.

"We won't be needing you now," the blond man said casually.

The young man's eyes swept past the broad shoulders to see the disarrayed Blair on the table and he assessed the situation immediately. When his eyes swung back to the larger man, they were glittering with insinuation. "I see what you mean," he said slyly. A playful elbow-in-the-stomach jab was implied by his smirking tone.

"Go ahead and bill Miss Simpson for your time."

"Yeah. Sure. Thanks." He winked at the blond man before picking up his leather bag of supplies and clumping down the stairs.

Blair watched as the blond man closed the door, but she was off the table before the latch clicked. No longer rendered senseless by her initial shock, she was now bristling with fury. "Who the hell are you? How dare you take advantage of me like this? Get out of here or I'm calling the police."

"On what? You've no telephone yet," he said reasonably. A broad grin split his mouth and showed her a beautiful set of gleaming white teeth. "The telephone company called today. An installer will be out the day after tomorrow."

"Who—"

"Sean Garrett. I'm your landlord. The carpenter and neighbor you don't want to be obligated to." He raked her disheveled appearance as she stood still, haphazardly wrapped in the sheet. "All you owe me is one thorough massage."

"You tricked me!" she shouted. Lightning flashed from her green eyes as she glared at him.

"No I didn't. I never said I was a masseur. You didn't give me a chance." He walked toward her and she found herself backing up instinctively. His size diminished the room which she had previously thought to be spacious. "Indeed, up to a point, I wasn't sure what service I was expected to perform."

The golden mustache quivered above the smiling mouth.

"You—"

"Let's see, you said you needed me now more than ever. You asked if I minded doing it on the kitchen table since the bed hadn't been made up. And you offered to undress. Now, what *is* a man supposed to think hearing words like those?"

He had continued to close in with that predatory gait as he spoke. She had backed up until she was against the kitchen countertop. Then he hitched a hip over the corner of the quilt-covered table, blocking off any route of escape. Feeling trapped, but knowing better than to concede any advantage, she stood as tall as she could and, despite her ridiculous costume, straightened her shoulders and raised her chin.

"You know good and well I mistook you for someone else. The decent thing to do would have been to identify yourself. I don't see how I can live here now knowing what kind of man my landlord is. As soon as you leave,"—she stressed that—"I'll carry my things back down to the car."

Whatever she expected of him, it wasn't the laughter that thundered out of his chest. His smile widened and he threw back his blond head in pure enjoyment. "So the heavenly body and innocent eyes are deceptive. Beneath them lurks the soul of a tigress. I like you, Blair Simpson."

"Well I don't like you," she shouted. "You're a liar and a sneak. Get out!"

"I never lied," he said with maddening calm while she thought she would burst with the anger roiling inside her.

"What would you call it?"

"I told you honestly that I didn't work for the Y. I said I was a free-lancer, which I am. I'm a contractor. You asked if I had enough clients and I said that you'd be surprised. I *do* have many clients. I buy old houses, restore them structurally, then sell them to wealthy city-dwellers who want a vacation home near the beach. So you see, everything I told you is the truth."

"But misleading."

He shrugged, his mouth tilting at the corners into a mischievous grin. "As I said, what's a man to do under such circumstances? When a beautiful woman offers to take off her clothes and lie down on the kitchen table, do you know any real man who would politely turn and leave?"

Thinking she'd shock him, she thrust out her chin and said defiantly, "As a matter of fact I do."

He wasn't impressed, as his nonchalant shrug testified. "I don't criticize anyone for his lifestyle. I only know what *my* sexual preferences are. And a beautiful woman wearing only a bedsheet, lying docile and pliant and begging for my touch appeals to me greatly."

"Begging! I didn't . . . the only reason I was letting you touch me is because I thought you were a professional masseur. Had I known—"

"Don't try to tell me you weren't enjoying it because I know better. You were practically purring. You weren't even aware of turning over and treating me to a look at all of you." He spoke the last words softly as he got off the table and took what few steps were necessary to stand directly in front of her. "From the back, you look like little more than a child. But from the front, for all your daintiness of figure, Blair Simpson, you are undeniably a mature woman."

His hands came up to cradle her jaw. She couldn't ward him off with her hands. They were occupied with holding up the sheet. "Don't," she said, trying uselessly to twist her head aside. She was ignored. His mouth was only a breath away from hers.

"I'll tell you something else. I'll blister your fanny if you ever again open your door to a strange man and let him come in. Don't you know what can happen to ladies when they act so carelessly?" The mustache made a brushing pass across her lips. "All kinds of perverts are walking the streets. If you had let one of them in instead of me, something terrible might have happened to you."

His lips pressed against hers and what little will she had remaining sifted through the barriers of her mind like the last grains of sand in an hourglass. His hands, cupping the back of her head, were as gentle as they had been while giving her the massage. His thumbs rotated hypnotically against her temples. She felt herself gravitating toward his body as though pulled by a magnet.

He dropped a few light kisses on her mouth before stepping away. Blair couldn't focus on him clearly, so dizzy was she made by the embrace and his untimely and cruel withdrawal. When her senses finally returned, the first thing that registered on her desire-clouded mind was his victorious grin. Any lingering passion she felt was immediately swapped for rage.

She shoved him away from her with one hand risking her hold on the sheet. "Get out!" she screamed. "You're the only pervert I've ever had the misfortune of meeting."

"I'll leave now," he said, turning away from her and navigating his way around the boxes to the front door. "But I'll have dinner ready at eight. Just come to the back door of the house and knock."

"Dinner! Are you suggesting that I have dinner with you after this?"

"I see no reason why not. Now that we know each other so well." The meaning behind his smile left nothing to the imagination.

"Good-bye, Mr. Garrett. You'll see me on the first of next month when my rent is due."

"I'll see you at my back door at eight or I'll come get you." Before she could respond he added quietly, "Pam told me about your knee injuries. I'm truly sorry you won't be able to dance for awhile."

Then he was gone and Blair was staring at the wooden door he'd quietly closed behind him.

"You mean you were lying there n-a-k-e-d with Sean Garrett's hands sliding all over your body?" Blair watched sadly as Pam Delgado popped another chocolate chip cookie into her mouth and chewed it lustily while her eyes were staring with wide incredulity at her friend.

"Yes. It was awful."

Pam laughed, nearly choking on the cookie. "Oh, the pits to be sure," she scoffed. "Who do you think you're fooling, ol' friend? Much as I love and adore my Joe, I'd probably be tempted to submit should Sean offer to give me a massage on the kitchen table and so would ninety-nine percent of the women in town."

Pam and her brood of five had descended on Blair an hour after Sean had left. Pam had assigned jobs to her four oldest children. Two were emptying boxes of books and records into the built-in bookshelves in the main room. One was folding towels and linens into the closet in the bathroom. The other was unpacking pots and pans into a kitchen cabinet. Pam and Blair were sitting at the table, talking over the clatter. The youngest Delgado, a boy a few months past his first birthday, was on his mother's lap, smearing himself with a soggy cookie.

"Well then, I'm one of that one percent who wouldn't. Pam, why didn't you tell me this man, who is my nearest neighbor and landlord, is a . . . a perverted—"

"He did something perverse?" Pam asked eagerly, dodging at the same time the bite of cookie the baby was foisting on her. "What?"

"No, he didn't do anything perverse," Blair said in vexation, standing to go to the countertop to pour more soda into Pam's near-empty glass. "The whole thing was perverted. He took advantage of me," she cried. "I was mortified."

Pam's eyes softened a bit. "Well I can see how you might be upset. But you've got to admit being taken advantage of by Sean isn't exactly a fate worse than death. I know women who'd—"

"Would you stop saying that please?" Blair asked, slightly irritated. "As you know I'm not like other women. They can have the macho types. I'm not impressed by Sean Garrett as being anything other than a scheming womanizer."

"But he's not," Pam came to his defense quickly. "Blair, he's one of the pillars of the community. He's successful in business, he's on the city council, a member of the school board—"

"My God! You mean he's got children?"

"No, no. He's never been married, but he's interested in all aspects of the community. In addition he's charming, and damned good to look at. Don't tell Joe, but I nearly ran the Volvo off in a ditch one day when I saw him working on a roof wearing nothing but a pair of shorts. Without a shirt he's—"

"Okay," Blair said, throwing up her hands in a gesture of surrender. "He's absolutely wonderful and I'm weird for not realizing how lucky I am that he made a complete fool out of me."

Pam's smile drooped. Reaching across the table, she covered Blair's hand with her own. "I'm sorry. Knowing how . . . well, how headstrong you are, I can see how you'd be angry that he duped you so easily. But, Blair, you have to admit that it's funny. Some of the things you said . . ." She couldn't hold back the laughter any longer and it bubbled out of her throat.

"Thanks a lot," Blair said, with a wry smile. "Traitor. Are you sure you aren't descended from Benedict Arnold?"

"Does his machismo make you nervous?"

"Whose? Benedict's?" Blair said in an attempt to avoid Pam's perceptive question.

"Sean's."

Blair laughed. "Of course not."

"I just wondered," Pam said with obvious off-handedness. She crimped the curls on the baby's head. "I mean, you haven't really been involved with a man since Cole."

Blair looked away. "No I haven't." Neither Pam nor anyone else knew the whole story of her relationship with Cole Slater and no one ever would. By tacit agreement, they'd never discussed it. If Pam harbored any curiosity about that segment of Blair's past, she was friend enough not to pry. For that Blair was grateful. Pam wasn't prying now. She was only providing a key should Blair want to open a closed door. She didn't. "Sean Garrett just isn't my type, that's all."

Pam laughed. "If you're a woman, he's your type."

Blair studied her friend who had gained too much weight with each successive child until the accumulation had carried her far beyond being pleasantly plump. "If you're so enchanted with Sean Garrett, why didn't you go after him instead of Joe?" Blair teased.

Pam spread her arms wide. "Because Joe loves me just the way I am." Her eyes sparkled happily. "And can he ever love!" she added with an exaggerated sigh. Her skin, which she had sense enough to protect from too many sunny days on the beach, was clear and smooth. Her hair, piled up on top of her head in a careless knot, was a summation of her philosophy of life. She looked happy and totally fulfilled, and Blair knew a pang of envy.

"I know you think I've let myself go to pot," Pam said with characteristic honesty. "I know I look like a blimp and no longer resemble the svelte dancer who fought every ounce. Don't think I don't look at you and get pea green with envy for your tiny figure. I do. Firm thighs, a flat stomach, and breasts that don't sag are history for me. But I'm happy, Blair. I've got Joe and the kids and I love them. I wouldn't trade places with anyone. I wouldn't trade places with you, glamorous career or no glamorous career."

Strident voices from the living room indicated that Andrew didn't approve of the way Mandy was doing her job. Mandy said she was going to tell Mama if Andrew didn't leave her alone. Andrew yelled, "Tattletale, tattletale."

The two women scarcely heard them. Blair was staring down at her hands and Pam was watching helplessly as she read the heartache on her friend's enviably youthful face.

"I wouldn't blame you for not wanting to trade

places with a thirty-year-old gypsy with banged up knees," Blair said forlornly.

"Your knees will heal and you'll be back dancing in no time."

"And if they don't heal? What then?"

"Then you'll do something else."

"I don't know anything else, Pam."

"Well, you'll learn something else. My Lord, Blair, you're beautiful and talented and the fact that you're thirty may be threatening if you want to be a professional dancer, but there are other things you can do that haven't even occurred to you yet. I know you're not stupid enough to think that your life is going to end now that you're thirty and may not be able to dance anymore."

"The life I *want* will be over."

"How do you know what you want? You've never known any other life but dance. Something wonderful may be in store for you that you couldn't even guess at. Do you think I thought, God let me be mugged that day in the park so I'd have to file a report with a cop named Delgado who had beautiful brown eyes and a wonderful laugh? That your knees are giving out may be the best thing that's ever happened to you."

Blair saw that arguing was useless, so she patted Pam's plump hand and said, "Maybe so," knowing full well that such was not the case.

With Pam helping and the children causing a minimum of chaos, they managed to unpack most of the boxes in the next hour. Pam sent the older children down the stairs with the empty boxes with instructions to put them into Sean's trash barrels.

"Can we go see Sean?" Mandy, the oldest girl, asked Pam.

"No. He's probably out working somewhere."

"His truck's here. So is his car," Andrew said. He was the oldest of Pam's children, just approaching nine.

Pam sighed. "Just for a minute then." Despite her warnings that they be careful on the stairs with the boxes, they raced down them.

"Andrew's got a terrible crush on you," Pam said. "He asked me the other day if I thought you were pretty. Usually he scorns females of any kind."

"I thought boys had their first crushes on their teachers."

"It's summertime," Pam said and they laughed.

When the two came bounding back upstairs they were slurping on Popsicles. "Sean gave them to us. He sent these to the others," Andrew explained, handing the other three Popsicles to his mother.

"Oh, let's hurry out of here or we'll drip all over Blair's floor," Pam said, quickly grabbing up the baby, her purse and car keys.

"Oh, yeah, I almost forgot," Andrew said to Blair just as his mother was shooing him out the door. "Sean said for you to dress casual tonight."

Pam stopped her frantic efforts to herd her children down the stairs and looked over her shoulder. "Tonight?" she asked on a high note.

"He has the mistaken idea that I'm going to eat dinner with him," Blair mumbled.

"You're not?"

"No!"

"Wanna bet?" Pam asked, winking before she turned to assist three-year-old Paul down the steps.

When Pam had first told her about the garage apartment, Blair had asked if it had a bathtub. One of the things the doctor said would help her knees was frequent soaking in hot baths. Pam had assured her it had one. Now, Blair was taking her first relaxing bath in the old-fashioned, deep, claw-footed tub and it felt wonderful. The tension that had been building since she first saw Sean Garrett standing on her threshold began to dissolve in the steamy water.

When the water finally began to cool, she stood up, reeling slightly. The hot water had weakened her and she realized that she hadn't eaten anything all day. She dried, noticing that her skin was smooth and fragrant with the residue of the lotion that Sean had massaged into it. Starting to pull on her oldest and most comfortable robe, she paused to reconsider. What if he carried out his threat to come get her when she didn't show up at his back door at the appointed time? Cursing him and her own culpability, she sacrificed the robe for a pair of jeans and a tank-top T-shirt, both old and well-worn if not as comfortable as the robe she'd intended to wear.

The package of chocolate chip cookies had been

virtually demolished, but the rest of the groceries Pam had brought by way of a housewarming gift lined the shelves of the cupboard and refrigerator. Blair was inspecting them when she heard the first footfall on the stairs.

"It can't be," she whispered. Her eyes flew to the clock and the digital readout told her it was 8:01. The heavy footsteps on the stairs grew ominously louder as they neared the top. "He won't bully me," she swore to herself as she marched across the living room with a militant stride. As soon as he knocked on the door, she flung it open, ready to do battle if necessary.

Her scathing refusal to join him for dinner died on her lips. He was anything but menacing. Instead he looked like a boy calling for his first date. He was dressed in a pair of jeans and a sport shirt. It was opened to the middle of his chest, revealing a carpet of curling golden hair over coppery skin. His hair was well brushed and picked up the glow from the soft porch light Blair had switched on earlier. His cheeks shone with a recent shave. His cologne was elusive but potent and did nothing to alleviate Blair's light-headedness due to hunger and the hot bath. In his hand he carried a green paper-wrapped bouquet of daisies.

"Hi."

"Hi." Her voice didn't sound like her own. The word was forced out of a throat swallowing convulsively.

"This is a peace offering for what I did this afternoon. Will you forgive me?" he asked penitently. She didn't answer, only stared at the flowers he was extending to her. "They really should be put in water," he said gently. He stepped forward and, like someone in a trance, she moved aside and allowed him to enter the room. His arm lightly grazed her breast. "Do you have a vase?"

"In . . . In the kitchen . . . I think," she stammered and went to the cabinet where she had put incidentals. There she found a slender, clear glass vase, filled it with water, and carried it into the living room to set on the coffee table.

He unwrapped the flowers and carefully arranged them in the vase with hands that looked too large to undertake such a delicate enterprise. But then Blair knew just how tender those hands could be.

"There. That looks terrific," he said, wadding up the green paper. He casually went to the pantry in the kitchen, opened the door, and dropped the ball of paper into the garbage can he'd correctly guessed would be there. "Everything's shaping up," he said as his eyes surveyed the room. The lamp's soft glow camouflaged some of the areas that hadn't come under her attention yet, and Blair had to agree that the room had a certain ambiance.

The walls were painted a soft beige, while the woodwork of the window frames, door frames, baseboards, and moldings around the ceiling were painted white. The windows were tall and wide and shuttered with white louvers.

"Have you tried the bed yet?" Sean asked, indicating the sofa.

"No," Blair said, shaking her head. "I made it up this afternoon, but I haven't uh, I . . . lain down on it."

"I hope it's comfortable," he said, ignoring the bed and studying her mouth. "When I bought furniture for this apartment, I wanted things that were simple and comfortable."

"Everything's fine."

"Good."

They stared at each other for an endless moment, then both looked away awkwardly. "I really am sorry about this afternoon," he said after a while. Only when Blair lifted her eyes to meet his gaze again did he continue. "I want you to understand that I'm not sorry it happened, or that I saw you that way, or that I touched you." His voice had the stirring bass vibrations of a fine cello. "I'm only sorry that you were embarrassed. It was a low trick I played on you and you had every right to be angry."

She tried to banish the words about his seeing and touching her and concentrate on his deception and her anger. Why had he approached her this way? She had built up an arsenal of rebukes, of condemnations, but she couldn't use them now that he was so meekly apologetic. He had robbed her of the one weapon she had—anger. That was another low trick.

"You're right. I was furious."

"I promise the next time I give you a massage, it will be with your full consent."

"I—" She was never allowed to tell him there wouldn't be a next time.

"That's a strange print," he said, looking over her shoulder.

She turned to see that he was looking at Harvey Edwards's *Hands*. "You're looking at it from the wrong angle," she said. She went to the brass-framed print that was leaning vertically against the wall and turned it horizontally. "It goes this way. I haven't had time to hang it yet."

"Oh, I see," he said, nodding. "Interesting, isn't it?"

"I love it, as I do most of his work." They studied the photograph that captured the arched torso of a ballerina being supported by a pair of masculine hands that defined strength, yet intimated sensitivity. "He photographs dancers. That's one of his, too." She indicated another print of a pair of well-worn faded pink toe shoes against a solid background of black. "It's called *Shoes*."

"Big on titles, isn't he?" Blair was intrigued by the way the lines around his eyes crinkled when he smiled. "Do you have a pair of shoes like that?"

She laughed. "Several hundred."

"How do you ever learn to wind those ribbons around your ankles and make them stay?"

"Practice. And the ribbons have to be sewn on just right."

"The shoes don't come with them already on?"

"No, you have to do it yourself. And it's bad luck for anyone but the ballerina to sew on her ribbons."

"I didn't know that."

During this whole inconsequential exchange

there was an important battle being waged. Their eyes competed against one another to see whose could take in and register the most information about the other in a given amount of time.

Her eyes noted the way his hair molded so nicely, yet disobediently, to his head; the way his mustache curved over his upper lip; the way the cleft in his chin punctuated the total masculinity of his face like a small exclamation point.

His eyes recorded the number of times her tongue nervously wet her lips; the way her hands moved in their own special ballet when she gestured; and how long her dark lashes were when she lowered them in an unconsciously seductive manner.

"Hungry?"

The question was so abrupt that Blair was ripped from her dazed inspection of him and brought back to the subject at hand. As though she'd been shot from a cannon, it took her a moment to orient herself, to gather her wits about her enough to say, "Mr. Garrett, I don't think it's a good idea for me to have dinner at your house. I appreciate your invitation but I—"

"Don't want to be obligated to your neighbors," he finished for her.

"Well, yes. That and—"

"You're afraid that I'll do something underhanded like I did this afternoon and put the make on you."

"No—"

"You're afraid I *won't* put the make on you?"

"No!" she fairly shouted in exasperation. His

piercing blue eyes were unnerving her. They kept wandering in the vicinity of her breasts. Why hadn't she put on a bra, or another top? "I'm not afraid of anything," she stressed, "but—"

"Gossip? Are you afraid that our having dinner together would jeopardize our reputations? You're right that in a town this size everyone knows everyone else's business, but I assure you I have more to lose than you. I'm known here. You're not. If I'm not concerned about gossip you shouldn't be."

"I'm not," she said, finally losing the tenuous grip on her temper. "I'm a grown woman, Mr. Garrett, who has lived alone for many years in New York City. I can take care of myself and I don't give a damn what the busybodies in this town think of me or what I do." She paused to heave in a breath.

"Then there's no reason for you not to have dinner with me. Are you ready?"

"Haven't you heard one word I've said?"

"I've heard them all and they're so much hot air. Are you ready?"

She threw up her hands in defeat. "All right," she shouted. "I'll go eat your dinner."

"Now see how easy that was?" he said with an amiable smile. "Come on." He ushered her toward the door.

"Just a minute. I need to comb my hair."

"No you don't. It looks good just like that."

"Well at least let me put some shoes on."

"Feet that have worn out that many pairs of toe shoes deserve one night off. Go barefoot."

"Very well," she said, giving in. "Come on."

"Just a minute. There is one other thing," he said as she turned toward him, a questioning frown on her face. "You forgot the light. I'm paying the utility bills, remember?"

He switched off the lamp on the table at the end of the sofa, plunging the room into darkness except for the glow of the porch light filtering through the shutters. Blair's hand was on the doorknob when she felt his hands settle lightly on her shoulders and turn her around. Her heart began beating in an irregular tattoo that affected her breathing as well.

"We have some unfinished business, Blair."

"I don't know what you mean, Mr. Gar—"

"Dammit! If you call me Mr. Garrett one more time, I'm going to remind you just how familiar we are," he warned in a low growl. The darkness didn't obscure the fire burning in his blue eyes. Each emphatic word caused a warm puff of breath to strike her face. The fingers wrapped around her upper arms were like velvet bonds, possessive and strong but warm and soft.

She swallowed. "What business, Mr. G . . . Sean?"

"This." His hands dropped from her shoulders to slide under her arms and close around her back. Spreading his fingers wide, he pulled her to him, pressing her against the rigidity of his large frame. "God, you're so tiny I feel like a child molester holding you this way," he murmured into her hair. He moved against her in a way that demonstrated a shocking insight into how to arouse her. "But I know that every inch of you is woman. I could almost encircle your waist with my hands, but it curves into the most feminine of hips." His large hands slid down the slender mounds, appreciating their firmness. "Your breasts are small but beautifully round and full. They respond to me. I've seen their response and now I can feel it against my chest." He peered down into her face.

She knew that her eyes were wide and unblinking. She knew that her lips were softly parted in disbelief. She knew that her expression showed how mystified she was that this was happening, that she was being held in the arms of a fiercely virile man. Most perplexing of all was that she wanted to be held.

"You're so small you make me feel like a bungling giant. I'll never hurt you, Blair. I promise. You'll tell me, won't you, if I ever hurt you?"

She could only nod dumbly. His mouth was teasing hers with feather-light kisses that barely qualified as such. She'd never been kissed by a man with a mustache and the masculine feel of it against her mouth was like an aphrodisiac that injected her with desire.

As his mouth grew more demanding and his tongue boldly glided along her lips, she resisted.

"Blair," he whispered urgently against her lips, "let me taste you. Open your mouth."

"No," she cried.

"Yes," he said adamantly and this time brooked no arguments. His mouth slanted over hers as he pulled her ever closer into him. Her back arched to mold her femininity against what it had been created to complement. Harmonizing sighs of gratification spiraled above them. Hands that had made futile attempts at extrication, now linked behind his neck. Softness conformed to hardness.

He conquered with tenderness and she yielded. He tickled the corners of her mouth with the tip of his tongue until her lips involuntarily relaxed. When he pushed it between her lips, his tongue didn't plunder, but persuaded. It flicked over her lips, her teeth, then gently pushed past that last barricade to explore the interior. He caressed with loving strokes each delicious discovery. He flirted with the tip of her tongue, then delved deeply. More than a kiss, it was an act of love.

When at last he pulled away, she leaned against him weakly. His hand smoothed over her hair and she thought it might be trembling slightly. Their breathing was that of two people who had climbed to a high altitude.

"I think we're doing things in reverse," he said. She felt his smile against her cheek. "We're having dessert before dinner."

Chapter 3

Engulfed by embarrassment over her unrestrained response to him, Blair avoided Sean's eyes as he escorted her down the outdoor stairs. She dreaded having to face him in full light once they reached his house across the brief expanse of lawn. The moment she entered the back door he held for her, though, her self-consciousness was swept away by enthrallment. His house was exquisite.

"Sean," she exclaimed, "this is beautiful."

"Do you like it?" he asked, obviously pleased by her reaction.

"Like it," she said, "what an understatement." He had led her into a screened back porch that was filled with wicker furniture, potted plants, and plump cushions piled onto the quarry tiled floor. Two ceiling fans with cane blades rotated overhead. The cushions on the natural wicker seats and on the floor were in a bold blue and brown print.

"When I bought the house, the porch was here, but it wasn't enclosed. I thought it would make a nice garden room. In the winter, I can weather secure it by sliding panes of glass into those frames."

"It's wonderful."

"Come see the rest."

His evident pride in the house was justifiable. As he walked Blair into the kitchen she caught her breath. Never having had more than a one- or two-room apartment in the city, she was aghast at the spaciousness of the room.

"I converted that old wood-burning stove so it could use gas."

The freestanding appliance was black iron and trimmed with brass. It matched a huge baker's rack of the same materials that covered another wall. Its shelves were loaded with brass and copper utensils, cookbooks, and plants.

"Did you decorate this yourself?" she asked.

"No. I only do the structural work. Then I turn the houses over to clients and they hire their own decorators. A friend helped me with this one."

Blair wondered about the identity of the "friend" with the impeccable taste as Sean led her through the rest of the lower floor. The dining room with its four-faceted bay window had been furnished with a round table worthy of the room. The living room boasted an antique European marble fireplace. Blair could see now why Sean would notice and appreciate her prints. The high ceilinged walls of the living room were splashed with prints of varying shapes, sizes and styles, yet all blended with the colors and textures found in the furniture, which was a congenial mixture of old and new.

A tiny powder room had been squeezed in under the polished oak staircase. One wall of the landing was stained glass, and Blair could only imagine how breathtaking it would be with sunlight behind it. Area rugs served to accent the aged patina of the parquet floors.

"Upstairs there are three bedrooms and three baths. We'll see them later. Right now I'm starving," he said, taking her arm and propelling her back toward the kitchen.

She was still mulling over what he'd said about seeing the bedrooms later, when they entered the bright kitchen and he said, "I hope you like chicken and wild rice."

"Yes. Can I help?"

"It's all done, but you can get the salad and dress it while I pour the wine."

"Okay."

She found a huge bowl of salad in the refrigerator and, selecting a vinegar and oil dressing out of the shelves in the door, poured a liberal amount onto the greens. She carried the bowl into the dining room where the table had already been set with informal china, linen napkins, and candles.

"Did you do all this yourself?" she asked Sean when he brought in the casserole and set it on a silver trivet.

He shrugged. "Yeah. I don't go to this much effort every night, you understand. I usually eat a bologna sandwich and drink a bottle of beer on the porch, but this is a special occasion."

She was standing beside her chair nervously. "Special?"

"I think so." He held her chair and she sat down, thankful that she had an excuse to let her knees collapse beneath her. Rather than moving to his chair immediately, he wrapped his arms around her shoulders and leaned down to place his mouth directly over her ear. "I could get accustomed to sharing meals with you." His mouth slid from her ear to the side of her neck, taking small love bites as it went. At the juncture with her collarbone, he kissed her, bathing the tender spot with his tongue. When he straightened at last, he slipped his finger beneath the shoulder of her tank-top and caressed her skin briefly before sitting down.

Blair, trying to restore some order to a world suddenly gone haywire, fumbled with her napkin as she placed it on her lap. "I feel like I'm underdressed," she said, tucking her bare feet under her chair.

"You're not. I'm only trying to impress you."

"I'm impressed. Where did you learn to entertain so graciously?"

He heaped her plate high with the seasoned rice and a boned chicken breast. "I guess I absorbed it by osmosis. My parents entertain quite a bit. Whatever I learned, I learned from my mother."

"Where do your parents live?"

"In New Jersey."

She passed him a basket of hot buttered bread after tearing off a generous hunk for herself. "What business is your father in?"

"He's retired." He changed the subject quickly by asking about her own family and they finished the meal over idle, chatty conversation.

When Pam had first told her about him, she had envisioned a near illiterate who made his living doing handiwork with a saw and hammer. Meeting him had altered that opinion considerably. Seeing the quality of the restoration on his house had elevated her assessment of his career, and through their dinner conversation, she learned that his interests were varied and many. He was intelligent, well-read, witty.

All the while she was enjoying his entertaining company, she searched for a flaw, something in him that repulsed her, some secret sin for which he could be despised. There was none. In every aspect, he was the most attractive man she had ever met. His very appeal shook the foundations on which her life was built. His smile made her want to flee, but at the same time she longed to bask in its golden warmth.

She declined his offer of dessert. "I'm not working out six hours a day," she said. "I'll have to start watching my calories."

She did accept a cup of coffee laced with Kahlúa and topped with thick whipped cream. He suggested they drink it on the porch and she quickly agreed. No lights were turned on as they settled themselves against the deep cushions of the furniture. A breeze off the ocean only a few blocks away filtered through the screened wall. Crickets chirped in the oak trees, and the fans overhead provided a steady humming lullaby.

Blair curled up in the corner of a small settee and tucked her feet beneath her. She sipped the foamy hot drink.

"You like?" he asked.

She smiled, licking whipped cream from the corner of her mouth. "I like."

He watched her in silence for a moment, then asked softly, "When did you start dancing?"

"When I was four."

"Four!"

She laughed. "That was when my mother enrolled me in my first ballet class. For my first recital, I was a pink and white cupcake."

"Yum-yum."

How he could fill such an innocent expression with such sexual implication amazed her. It disturbed her that in the darkness of the room and the flickering shadows caused by the circling fans, she couldn't tell the direction of his eyes. She quickly picked up her story.

"I've danced ever since. It's more than a career. It's a way of life that no one except another dancer can understand. We all eat, sleep, and breathe dance. We go without lodging and food to pay for classes. When we're not working in a show, we wait tables, do anything, to support ourselves. But we never sacrifice our classes. If someone's broke, he moves in with someone else until better times come along. It's a campy way of life. I guess that's why we're called gypsies. We carry our livelihoods around in canvas bags—smelly leotards, mended tights, worn-out shoes, leg warmers, ointments."

"But you've been successful. Pam's touted the many shows to your credit."

"I've been lucky, yes."

"Lucky, hell. You're good."

She smiled at him. "I'm good, but always striving to be better."

"Didn't you ever want to pull out of the chorus and be the star?" he asked.

"If you could hear my singing voice you'd know that would be a pipe dream. I couldn't even fake it. After years of voice and acting lessons, I recognized the hopelessness of playing a lead. And strangely enough I wasn't really interested. Love of applause wasn't my driving force, but rather love of dance. I was content to be the first dancer behind Liza Minnelli saying, 'Gee, that's super,' and other profound lines of dialogue like that."

"That should have won you a Tony," he laughed. But his eyes were serious, staring into the bottom of his cup at the dregs of the coffee he whirled round and round in a miniature whirlpool. Almost too casually he asked, "In all this moving in and out with people, was there ever anyone you lived with for an extended period of time?"

A year—would he consider that an extended period of time? A heartbreaking year, but one with rare moments of joy and sharing that made it worthwhile. She knew what he was asking—Had she ever lived with a man? Had there been a man in her life? "Yes." She answered him truthfully. "I lived with a man named Cole Slater for awhile. That was several years ago."

"And?" he asked when she didn't expand on that.

"And since then I've lived alone."

"I see."

He didn't, but she wasn't going to enlighten him. "I'll help you with the dishes," she said briskly. She unfolded from her relaxed position and picked up the cup and saucer she'd set on a glass-topped wicker table.

"I'll let you," he said jovially, following her into the kitchen.

They decided it would be expedient if she rinsed the dishes and stacked them in the dishwasher and let him put things away as only he would know where to put them. She was neatly folding a dish towel when he came up behind her and closed his arms around her waist, hugging her to him. The back of her neck knew the sweet nuzzling of his mustache and mouth.

"If our reputations are shot to hell already, we've

nothing to lose by really giving them something to talk about." He nibbled at her earlobe gently, his tongue batting against it playfully.

Softly, she gasped his name, "Sean . . ."

"Hm?" His hands scooted up her ribs to coast over her breasts. He took her indistinguishable murmur as consent and held her breasts gently in his palms. "Oh, God, Blair, you feel better than I imagined. So soft and full, so . . ." His mouth opened over her neck for a kiss that involved all of his mouth. His inquisitive fingers stroked and the cotton knit of her top couldn't contain the firm contraction of her nipples. "Yes, yes," he whispered harshly.

Only then did she realize that she was grinding her hips against his middle and that he needed no further encouragement. His arousal was firmly apparent against the cushion of her hips. Shocked at her own abandon, she tried to pry herself away from him, but was stayed by a hand stroking downward to insinuate itself under her top. The snap on her jeans was no deterrent and was deftly opened. Then that boldest of hands was flattened over her navel, exploring its perimeter with audacious fingers, fingers that were brazen enough to move ever lower, to toy with the elastic top of her bikini panties. When one slipped beneath that demarcating line, alarm bells pealed loud and clear through the fog of passion that swamped her and Blair broke free, whirling away from him. Her eyes were wide and her lips trembled uncontrollably as she faced him like a frightened doe.

"No, Sean." Her hair rippled around her as she shook her head emphatically.

"Why?" His chest heaved in an effort to still his rapid breathing. The pupils of his eyes were dilated, almost obscuring the blue irises.

"Why?" she repeated on a shuddering expulsion of air. "Because we only met today for one reason."

"What does that have to do with anything? I knew from the moment I saw you I wanted you. And admit it or not, you want me just as much."

"I don't," she shouted, hurriedly resnapping her jeans and pulling her tank-top down over the waistband. She was tempted to cover her breasts with her hands to hide their pointed agitation from his avid eyes. She willed them to relax. They refused. Her whole body, which had been trained to obey each command of her brain, had rebelled. It betrayed her with throbbing reminders of his touch, with aching pleas that it craved what he could provide.

Summoning what strength she could she said heatedly, "I made it clear from the first that I'm here temporarily. I don't have the time or the inclination to become involved."

"Oh . . ." His expletive was strained through his teeth. For long moments he stood with hands on his hips, glaring at her from across the narrow space that separated them. For all his gentleness, Blair knew then that Sean Garrett had a temper that could flare to life when properly provoked. The fire in his eyes now wasn't so much lust as it was anger.

His ire only increased hers. Wasn't she permitted

to say no? Did he think she was only so much putty in his hands, waiting to be molded however he saw fit? A spineless female panting for his attention? After hearing a happily married woman like Pam expound on his sex appeal, she shouldn't be surprised by his arrogance. He couldn't be completely oblivious to his virile attraction. Well for once it would be rejected.

Raising her chin stubbornly, she said, "It all boils down to this. I don't want to go to bed with you, Mr. Garrett." With that inspired exit line, she turned on her heel and stalked through the kitchen. He caught her at the back door.

Before she had time to react, he scooped her up in his arms. "What do you think you're doing?" she asked haughtily as he pushed through the screened door and started across the grassy lawn.

"As long as I'm here there's no reason for you to climb those stairs. You may not *think* you need anybody, and I know you'd never ask for help, but I can at least save your knees that much effort."

He carried her up the stairs without any exertion and deposited her on the top step. With as much dignity as she could muster she said, "Thank you for dinner."

Before the last word had completely left her mouth, it was being kissed by hot, fervent lips. Bands of steel in the form of arms wrapped around her and pressed her into a body that radiated carnal energy. Her mouth wasn't prepared for the onslaught of his and could find no strength to resist when his tongue plunged inside.

Then just as suddenly as the storm broke, it subsided. The arms relaxed, holding her no less firmly, but more tenderly. His tongue made slow dipping forays into her mouth that left her breathless.

Sensing her acquiescence, his hand moved from her back to lightly cup her breast. His thumb skated along the undercurve and she heard her own moan of rising passion. As he coaxed her tongue into his mouth and sucked it gently, his thumb brought her nipple to a hard pebble of need. This torment went on and on until Blair was inundated with blind desire, moving against his hard body mindlessly, seeking fulfillment for the emptiness deep inside her.

She swayed drunkenly as he pulled away. Were it not for his hands on her upper arms, she would have toppled down the stairs. There was no smile on his face now, only set lines of stubborn resolution. "Like hell you don't want to go to bed with me, *Miss Simpson*."

Two mornings after she'd heard those words, she was still seething over them. She had avoided leaving the apartment the day after having dinner with Sean because of the fear of meeting him in the yard. Pam had loaned her the family's extra car indefinitely, but she really had nowhere to go. After she finished arranging the apartment to her satisfaction, she had spent the day as the doctor had advised her to spend most of her days—reclining with her legs elevated. She'd read, watched two old movies on the portable television set she'd brought with her from the city, ate when she was hungry, and napped.

She knew when Sean's battered truck lumbered into the driveway between her apartment and his house, but she refused to even look out the window to catch a glimpse of him. Yet when he left in his Mercedes in the early evening, she couldn't help but wonder where he was going and with whom. That he hadn't yet returned by the time she fell asleep made her unaccountably angry—both at him and at herself for caring.

The second morning, she had awakened cross with herself for letting a man like Sean Garrett bother her. She'd be here six months. Despite her threats to move out and find another place, she knew she wouldn't do it. Apartments like this were too hard to come by. And why should she let problems with her landlord force her to live somewhere she'd loathe? Nor was she going to live like a phantom, sneaking in and out at times when she was unlikely to run into him. She'd live like a sane, mature adult, which she'd seemed to have forgotten she was since meeting Sean Garrett. *That* was subject to change starting today.

She restored her bed into a sofa, then walked into the kitchen and bent down to take the teakettle out of the lower cabinet. With no more movement than required to do these two small chores, she knew that her muscles had become soft and her joints stiff with just one day's inactivity.

Donning a pair of pink tights, ballet shoes, a black leotard, and a pair of blue leg warmers, she went to the area in the large room near the windows. She'd purposefully left this space empty. Slowly and methodically she began to do her stretching exercises. She was into the second set of *pliés* when she heard someone on the stairs. A moment later he knocked on the door.

When she opened it, she was braced to face Sean, but breathed a sigh of relief when she saw it was the man from the telephone company.

"Miss Simpson?"

"Yes, come in."

She moved aside and he entered the room carrying a roll of cable and a rectangular box. "One desk slimline, ivory, push-button," he said, consulting an order he held in his hand. He was a young man in his early twenties with long hair and bright smiling eyes.

"Yes."

"Where do you want it?"

She indicated a low table at the end of the sofa. "I thought here."

He surveyed the area clinically. "That should do it. I can attach it to that baseboard under the window and run the cord under the rug. That way you won't be tripping on it. How's that?"

"That's fine."

He went about his work, making several trips back and forth to his truck. "Why don't you leave the door open?" Blair called to him. "That way you can come in and out even with your hands full."

"Thanks."

Unself-conscious of her attire but knowing she

shouldn't cool down too quickly, she pulled on a shirt and tied the tail in a knot at her waist. She left it unbuttoned and rolled the sleeves to her elbows. She went into the kitchen to brew a pot of tea while the telephone company man told her that he was a student at NYU who was only working as an installer during the summer. He was majoring in marketing.

He was finished with the installation by the time the tea was brewed. "Would you care for some tea?" she asked hospitably.

He hedged. "Got a Coke?"

She laughed. "Coming up." She filled a glass with ice and Coke and handed it to him. He drained it before taking a breath.

"Are you some kind of dancer?" he asked, looking down at her shoes.

"Yes. I dance professionally."

"No kiddin'! How about showing me a few steps?"

"How about you clearing out?"

Two surprised victims came under Sean's baleful gaze as they whipped their heads toward the deadly voice. The young man standing beside Blair swallowed a lump of fear.

"I . . . I was just about to go," he stuttered.

"Don't let us keep you."

The young man set the glass on the tabletop, but it fell over to send ice cubes scuttling across the varnished surface. Hastily he uprighted the glass, chunked the ice cubes back in it, and nervously dried his hand on his denim-clad thigh. He backed away to gather up his equipment.

Too angry to speak until now, Blair said to him, "Thank you for the telephone."

"You bet. If you have any trouble call m . . ." He darted a cautious look in Sean's direction. "Call us," he amended. He squeezed past Sean's looming bulk and scampered down the stairs as though grateful to escape with his life. Sean slammed the door shut behind him.

Fists digging into her hips, Blair faced him down when he turned around. "Well I hope you're happy with yourself. You succeeded in bullying a perfectly harmless boy."

"Boy my ass. And how do you know he was harmless? Didn't I warn you about letting strange men into this place while no one else is around?"

"My mother has warned me about that since I was six years old. I don't need you to keep harping on it. Besides he wasn't a 'strange man.' I knew he was from the telephone company. All I had to do was look at his big truck with the bright blue and yellow stripes down its side." She was shouting at full voice, letting off some of the steam that had been collecting inside since he had insulted her with that torrid kiss the night before last.

His volume was no more monitored than hers. "If he were a sterling character, he could be tempted to fall from grace after seeing you. Have you looked in a mirror? Or are you so used to prancing around like that, that you didn't realize what a come on it is?"

Truly perplexed, she glanced down at herself. Raising her eyes back to his she said loftily, "These happen to be my work clothes. And I wasn't *prancing*. I was doing some exercises when he arrived, and yes, I am accustomed to wearing leotards and tights."

"Of course you have no idea what those woolly things—"

"Leg warmers."

". . . what those leg warmers do for your body," he finished sarcastically. "It's pure coincidence that they come to just above your knees and draw attention to the top of your thighs. Not to mention that the legs of that leotard are cut up so high you might as well not have anything at all over your tight little rear. Oh, I'm sure our sweet boy didn't notice any of that when you opened your door to him dressed like that." As he talked, he made slow progress into the room until he stood within an arm's reach of her.

"As a matter of fact," she ground out, "I wasn't dressed like this when he came in." With frustrated fingers she worked at the knot at her waist until it fell free. "I didn't have this shirt on." She peeled off the shirt and flung it aside, baring to his livid eyes the deeply scooped neck and thin shoulder straps of her leotard.

His eyes riveted on her impertinent breasts that strained against the black cloth stretched over them like a second skin. His breath was vacuumed in sharply. Then his arm shot out and he clamped a hand around the base of her neck. He hauled her against him with a movement so swift and sudden that it drove the breath out of her body on impact.

Ineffectually she pummeled him with her fist as his mouth cemented with hers. His other arm went around her waist and he lifted her against him to carry her squirming, struggling form to the sofa. His knee sank into the cushions as he lay her down and followed with his own body. One heavy leg lay across hers, pinning them down while his hands trapped her head and held it still for his kiss.

During it all, even while she writhed against him and fought with all her strength, he kept his promise. He didn't hurt her.

When she began to weaken, the pressure of his mouth decreased until he was sipping at her lips, laving them with his tongue. She whimpered her last protest and surrendered to her thirst. He didn't delay in spearing his tongue into her mouth and claiming it as his own. He cradled her cheek in one of his large palms while the other hand went undetained to her breast and fondled it reverently.

"I've become a jealous maniac, Blair," he said into her mouth. "I don't want any other man looking at you." His hand slid between her flesh and the elasticized leotard, pulling it down until her breast was free of its confinement.

"No," she groaned at his misplaced possessiveness. "You have no . . . say . . . over who . . ." Then she groaned for a different reason. He'd be so disappointed. Dancers were characteristically flat chested and—

"My God," he whispered.

The awesome tone of his voice forced her eyes to open. He was studying her with careful attention to detail. "What a gorgeous color you are, Blair. Delicate." His blond head rested against her chest. For a moment she thought she imagined the light caresses, until she felt the air cooling against the damp skin. Then all too keenly she felt the finessing of his tongue. "Delicate and so sweet," he murmured against her.

"No, no, Sean. Please . . ."

"Why? Tell me why." His tongue caressed elusively until she was surrounded by the hot, honeyed trap of his mouth.

Her fingers plowed through the thick mane of his hair and held his head secure. He drew on her with a sweetness that made her want to weep. "Because . . . because . . . there's no room in my . . . life for this. I don't . . ."

He levered himself above her to pierce her with his laser-beam eyes. "You don't want anything or anybody to interfere with your career, is that it?"

"Yes," she said fiercely and didn't know if her desperation stemmed from her wanting him to accept that fact or from the withdrawal of his mouth from her breast.

"When your legs heal, you'll go back and nothing will stop you."

"Yes."

"You don't want to build a life here."

"No."

"And you don't want anyone in your life. You don't want this?" He moved against her in a way that blatantly stated his meaning. The thin leotard and tights were no protection from his aroused sex.

"No."

"You don't need it." He pressed himself against her more firmly.

"No," she sobbed.

"And you're a liar. You need me right now so badly that you're in pain."

His knee gently prized her legs apart and he lay atop her, gathering her under him as though to harbor her from any and all harm. "You're aching, Blair. Let me heal you," he whispered passionately. Contrary to her protestations, her body adjusted to his with a silent entreaty and they clung together.

It was then they heard the rapid knocking on the door.

"Shhh," Sean hissed into her ear. "Please don't answer." He squeezed his eyes shut as though to block out the intrusion. His expression was agonized.

"Aunt Blair, it's me, Andrew," a high, piping voice called. "Aunt Blair, are you here?"

Chapter 4

Sean's head dropped to his chest as though a hinge at his neck had let go. Breath filtered through his teeth in a long, low sigh. Slowly he eased away from her.

"Aunt Bl—"

"Coming, Andrew," she called shakily as she fumbled to raise the strap of her leotard. Her eyes refused to meet Sean's as she swung her legs off the couch and hurried to the door. "Hi!" she said with a false gaiety as she pulled open the door.

"Were you in the bathroom or something?" Andrew asked with childlike candor.

"Uh, no. S . . . Sean and I were trying out my

new telephone. Remind me to give you the number to give your mom."

At mention of his hero's name, Andrew's dark eyes swept the room. "Hi, Sean," he said brightly and skirted past Blair into the room.

"Hi, there." Sean extended his palm and Andrew slapped it with his fingers.

"How did you get over here?" Blair asked.

"I walked," Andrew said proudly. "I know a shortcut. Mom sent me to tell both of you that she's having a party tonight. Well, it's not really a party, just some people coming over for steaks, ya know? Anyway you're both supposed to come at eight o'clock. She said you could drive over together and save gas."

"Great," Sean said.

"I don't know," Blair said at the same time.

She could hug the boy in gratitude that he had prevented something disastrous from happening. Whatever had possessed her to let things go so far? Sean's hands, his lips, had seduced her into a realm where she didn't even recognize herself. His touch was lethal and yet she responded to it each time, though vowing she would not. Her lack of control whenever he was around was frightening.

The first time he had kissed her, she had been shocked by the potency of his kiss and the overwhelming effect it had on her. The tantalizing power of his lips, the intrusion of his tongue into her mouth, had all been new to her. She had been kissed many times, yes, but never with such dominance. Always before she had remained detached, barely tolerant of the man who was slaking a desire she couldn't understand. She understood now. For what had been inconceivable only a few days ago was now familiar. The nuances of Sean's mouth had become like an addiction to her. Knowing it was dangerous, even deadly, she craved more in increasing amounts and frequent doses. Each time he kissed her, he created a gnawing need that could well destroy her life's blueprint.

More alarming than her own physical susceptibility was his possessive attitude toward her. Who had given him the right to watch over her, to say who she could and couldn't invite into her own apartment, what she should or shouldn't wear? She had lived thirty years without his protection and she didn't think she'd need it for at least thirty more.

After the debacle of a few moments ago, spending the evening with him was out of the question. "I'm awfully tired, Andrew, my legs have been hurting this morning, and I'm sure I won't be missed."

Andrew turned to her, his eyes peering out from bangs in need of a trim. "You gotta come, Aunt Blair. Mom said she was giving the party to introduce you to people."

"Yeah, Blair, you gotta go," Sean added tauntingly.

She read the challenge in his eyes. His grin was salacious, daring. If she backed out of the invitation, he would see it as cowardice and he would be absolutely right. She blessed him with a withering look. "Okay, Andrew," she said through tight lips. "Tell your mom I'll be there."

"Super. She said Mandy and me could stay up until eight-thirty if we promised not to get in the way."

"Mandy and I," Sean corrected him. "Say, I could use a helper today. I'm working on a house on the beach. Would you be interested in earning a dollar or two?"

"Gee, Sean, that'd be great!"

Sean smiled. "Go call your mom and tell her where you'll be. The back door is open. I'll meet you in the kitchen. We'll need a cooler of water on a hot day like today."

"Okay. See ya tonight, Aunt Blair," Andrew called as he dashed out the door and bounded down the stairs in his excitement.

As soon as the boy was out of earshot, Sean turned to Blair. "Are your legs really hurting?"

Prepared to light into him about his high-handedness with her, Blair was defeated once again by his gentleness. She shrugged indifferently. "A little."

"Maybe you should call your doctor."

"No," she snapped. Then thinking that sounded too defensive, she said, "I didn't do much yesterday. I just need to work some kinks out with exercise."

"I think you should rest them."

"Well I didn't ask to hear what you think, did I? And whatever you do think is of no interest to me."

"Isn't it?"

"No." Her breasts rose and fell with her growing irritation. She was furious with him for always being so damnably right and furious with herself for always being on the defensive. "What happened here," she indicated the sofa with an impatient gesture, "was a mistake and won't be repeated. And it certainly doesn't give you license to pry into my life."

"I wasn't prying. I was only expressing concern."

"Well I don't need your concern."

"Yeah, I know. You don't need anybody."

"I'm glad you finally got the message. Now you can stop pestering me all the time."

"You don't like my company?"

"Not particularly. You're overbearing. I don't like aggressive men."

"You don't like it when I kiss you?"

"No."

"You don't like it when I caress you?"

"No," she cried, hoping the strident sound of her voice would drown out the questions he asked in a soothing tone.

"When I touch and kiss your breasts?"

"No!"

"You're lying again, Blair."

He was right. Even now her body was quivering with remembrance of his embraces. She longed to feel again the silky caress of his mustache on her flesh. But she'd be damned before she'd say that out loud to him. Forcing the sensuous thoughts from her mind she faced him, her whole body crackling with anger. Again he was too quick for her. He turned the tables.

"Relax, Blair. I've never forced myself on any woman. If my caresses are repulsive to you, then I won't touch you as a lover again. However, I see no reason why we can't be friends. I'll pick you up just before eight. In the meantime, *as a friend*, I recommend you rest your legs."

Then he was gone before she was able to utter one word of objection.

The sounds of loud conversation and laughter reached them as they walked up the sidewalk to the Delgados' house. "I guess the party is already in full swing," Sean said.

"I guess so."

He had arrived at her door just as he had said, a few minutes before eight. She was ready except for her jewelry. He waited inside the threshold as she put pearl studs in her ears and misted herself with fragrance.

She couldn't have criticized his manners. They were above reproach. Glancing at him surreptitiously in the mirror, she saw that he wasn't looking at her, but was fiddling with the brass doorknob. "This is loose. Remind me to fix it," and "That's a pretty dress," were spoken with the same degree of emotion.

"Thank you." The white eyelet halter dress fit tightly through the bodice and waist to swing full and loose to just below her knees. With it she wore a pair of strappy gold sandals that wrapped around her ankles. Both the hemline of the skirt and the sandal straps around her ankles accented the perfect formation of her calves.

If his fingers touched her bare back as they descended the stairs, she was certain it was only for courtesy's sake. He ushered her into the Mercedes and then launched into a tale about Andrew racing across the beach with a sack of nails. When he tripped in the deep sand, the nails went flying and it had taken him and Sean a half hour to sift through the sand to see that all were picked up.

"I only hope we didn't miss one and someone finds it for us with his heel," he said.

Blair was laughing when she replied, "So do I. Was he worth the dollar you paid him?"

"I had to pay the little con man two dollars. Inflation."

By the time they pulled in front of Pam's house, she had relaxed her guard. Apparently Sean had taken her at her word. He was behaving as a good friend and not as a would-be lover.

Pam greeted them with warm, effusive hugs. "The guest of honor is here," she called to the other guests who were milling around the hors d'oeuvre trays strategically placed around the cluttered room.

They were swarmed by those wishing to be introduced to Pam's friend whom many of them considered a celebrity. Blair gave Pam an I-don't-believe-this look when she realized her friend had colored her successful career to sound more grandiose than it was. She was aware, too, of Sean being greeted just as enthusiastically as she. The women simpered; the men spoke deferentially.

Amidst all the confusion, Blair stooped to kiss each little pajamaed Delgado before he or she was aimed in the direction of the bedrooms with a stern command to go to bed.

"Those kids!" Pam exclaimed when the last was seen disappearing into the hallway. "They're enough to make me want to abstain."

Just then Joe Delgado, wearing his perpetual grin and a chef's apron with "This Cook Knows How to Sizzle" printed on it, came up to them and encircled his wife with his arms just below her breasts. "Well, not completely *abstain* . . ." Pam said suggestively to Blair and winked lewdly. The two women laughed.

"Did I miss something?" Joe asked good-naturedly and greeted Blair with a kiss on the cheek and Sean with a hearty handshake. He was as lean and wiry as his wife was plump and soft. "The room is coming along great, Sean. We can't wait."

"What room?" Blair asked, now feeling that she'd missed something.

"Sean's adding a playroom onto the back of the house. Did I forget to tell you?" Pam asked.

"Yes," Blair said, stealing a glance up at Sean who stood as close as he could without actually touching her.

"Oh, we can't wait for it to be finished. I'll show you later. First there are a dozen people wanting to meet you."

For the next few minutes Blair fielded the myriad

questions hurled at her. Had she ever danced with Baryshnikov? Was a ten-year-old too young to start *pointe*? Did she adhere to any special diet to stay so thin? How much did she weigh anyway? Was it true she and Pam had once taken classes with Juliet Prowse? Were her nails real or were they sculptured? Would she even consider auditioning the players for the PTA benefit talent show?

Over that question, she stammered a polite promise to think about it. She almost jumped when large hands cupped her shoulders. "What would you like to drink?" Subconsciously, only for a precious moment, she leaned against the tall, strong frame behind her. The bare skin on her back met the texture of his navy summer weight sportscoat and the smooth coolness of his pale blue cotton shirt. She wasn't even aware that she tilted her head to the side to better feel the mustachioed lips against her ear.

"White wine on the rocks," she whispered, trying unsuccessfully to listen to the lady from the PTA expounding on the value of their talent show. Blair's shoulders were squeezed lightly before Sean moved away.

Minutes later he was back with an icy glass of sparkling wine. The woman's incessant chatter hadn't flagged for one moment.

"Blair, I think Pam's looking for you. She's in the kitchen."

"Excuse me," Blair said graciously before letting Sean steer her away from the woman.

"Thanks," she said out of the corner of her mouth.

"That broad would bore a statue," he said, leaning down to whisper in her ear. "She pulled the same thing with me a few years ago. Since I was Irish she thought it would be so nice if I'd sing 'Danny Boy' in their talent show."

Blair nearly choked on her sip of wine. Tears of mirth filled her eyes. "You're kidding," she said on a laugh.

"I wish I were."

"And did you sing 'Danny Boy'?"

He scowled darkly, lowering the thick brows over his brilliant eyes. "I bought her off with a hundred-dollar check."

They were laughing when they entered the chaos of the kitchen. Pam was taking bowls of potato salad and cole slaw from the refrigerator. "Oh, I'm glad you two wandered in. Sean, go show Blair the new room."

"Don't you need any help?" Blair asked.

"Not this minute. Go on. Have a good time."

They exited through the sliding glass door leading off to the patio. The aroma of charcoaled meat wafted toward them. Joe was flipping large slabs of steak on the grill.

"You *look* like you know what you're doing," Sean said teasingly.

"Rare, medium rare, well done," Joe enumerated, pointing out each section of the grill with his long-pronged fork, then taking a large gulp of beer.

"Lay off the beer until my steak's cooked," Sean

said. Joe saluted him with the fork. They laughed and strolled to the other end of the patio. "Watch your step."

Sean guided her through the skeletal wooden framework of the new room. "This is going to be a playroom?" Blair asked, her eyes scanning the bare concrete foundation.

"Yes. Over there will be a fireplace. Here, bookshelves and a built-in desk, should any of the children ever feel inclined to study," he said, smiling. "We're even going to install a small refrigerator along with a television set."

"Sounds terrific."

"I'm going to skylight it," Sean said, gazing up at the uncovered rafters overhead. "That'll save electricity, because I don't think the kids will be conscientious about turning off lights. I'm going to use—" He broke off and turned to her suddenly. "You really aren't interested in this, are you?"

"Yes I am." She was. She discovered that she liked the enthusiasm in his voice when he spoke about his work. His hands, gesturing descriptively, were eloquent. They had felt so warm on the bare skin of her shoulders. Reassuring. Comforting. "The kids are going to love it."

"I think Pam and Joe will too. Theoretically with all the kids in here, it will give them some privacy."

"I can imagine that their moments of privacy are few and far between."

He chuckled. "They couldn't be too hard to come by or there wouldn't be so many kids."

She joined his laughter as she looked up at him, and then suddenly, at the same time, their laughter broke off. The moment had become intensely intimate. Moonlight streamed in through the rafters overhead, casting his face in deep shadows as he looked down at her. She couldn't discern his expression, she only knew that he was studying her.

The moonlight that crowned his light colored hair bathed her face with a silvery glow. Sean longed to run his fingers over the glossy strands of her hair sleeked back into a classic ballerina's bun on her neck. His lips were starved for a taste of her mouth, moist and pink in the shimmering light. They longed to roam to her dainty ear with that beguiling pearl that almost matched the luminescence of her skin. His eyes traveled the path of the moonlight until it disappeared into the shadowy cleft between her small breasts. Imagination placed his tongue there and he could all but taste the warmth he knew he would find.

Fantasies filled his head. He could see again the shell-pink crest of her breast. He could feel again its velvet-button texture against his tongue. He could hear again her throaty purrs of pleasure as he had indulged his hunger for her taste.

In years, he didn't remember wanting a woman as he'd wanted Blair from the first time his eyes had encountered hers. Since then he had been single-minded in his daydreams. His body ached for hers. That made no damn sense at all. She wasn't the type he usually preferred. Because of his own size, he had commonly dated taller women, with generous figures.

To him Blair seemed like a doll. But a doll that lived and breathed and moved and was capable of quenching the fire in his loins that constantly mocked him.

It was all wrong and he knew it. Once, he had made grave errors in judgment and they had cost him everything. He had come away with a sounder insight into life's priorities and had managed to re-establish himself. He was now successful in all but one area of his life. He had no one to share it with. So far he'd found no one he'd risk sharing his life with. Love was so often dependent on things going right. When something went wrong . . .

Blair Simpson had her own problems to cope with. She was undergoing a crisis that she would have to confront. He didn't need her in his life. That would only complicate things. And she claimed not to need him.

Yet now, standing here in the moonlight, desire stampeded through his body. He wanted nothing more than to kiss away her insincere protests, to clasp her to him and bury himself deep inside her, begging her to relieve him of his agony.

The fierceness of his musings must have shown in the rugged planes of his face for she said his name tentatively. He shook his head to clear it, then drained the contents of his cocktail glass. "Yeah, I, uh, guess we ought to rejoin the others."

Blair had taken only a few sips of her wine. Her fingers were stiff with cold. She had clenched them around the glass as though it were her last handhold on sanity. Sean stepped aside and ushered her back across the patio. Joe was still at the grill, deep in discussion now with a defense attorney about crime on the streets.

Pandemonium had broken out in the kitchen. Pam was listening to first one offspring and then the other as they offered conflicting accounts of a pillow fight. A third child was wailing, tears rolling down her cheeks. Pam was fishing ears of corn out of a vat of boiling water and placing them on a platter.

Despite the children's obvious disobedience and Pam's anxiety, Sean and Blair burst out laughing. "What's going on?" Sean asked.

"I think they're just too excited to go to bed." She looked down at the children threateningly. "I'm going to call Daddy and he'll be mad."

They gave about as much credence to that warning as they had to the others. "Why don't you let me put them to bed?" Blair offered.

"But you're my guest," Pam protested.

"I'm your friend and you've got your hands full. Come on, kids, enough of this," Blair said firmly enough to get their attention. "Andrew, *march*," she said, pointing an imperious finger in the direction of the bedroom. "Come on, Mandy."

"I'll get this one," Sean said, picking up little Paul and heaving him over his shoulders to straddle his head. Paul whooped in glee and grabbed a handful of Sean's blond hair.

"I didn't volunteer you, too," Blair said as they trooped out of the kitchen, taking the back hallway that led to the two bedrooms the children shared.

"I couldn't let you take on the whole regiment."

As the two bedrooms were connected by a door, Blair and Sean were able to tuck everyone into their respective beds while keeping an eye on those already under the covers. The baby was the only one already asleep. He was still confined to a crib. The two girls slept in a double bed in the room with the baby. The two boys slept in bunk beds in the other. Since Andrew was the older, he had the top bunk.

"Set a good example for your little sister and go to sleep now," Blair whispered to Mandy. "Let your mom and dad enjoy their party. Okay?"

"Okay," she said, yawning. Angela, somewhere around four if Blair remembered correctly, was already drifting off. "Will you leave the lamp on?"

"Mandy is a baby, Mandy is a baby," Andrew chanted from his bunk.

"Cool it, Andrew," Sean said sternly.

"Well she is," Andrew said petulantly. "She has to sleep with Angela. I don't want anybody mashing me while I'm asleep."

"Mommy and Daddy sleep in a bed together," Mandy protested.

"No one else gets to sleep with them and we can't go in their room at night unless it's lightning and thundering," Angela contributed sleepily.

Blair met Sean's laughing eyes across the room and then darted them back to the girls.

"We can't go in their room on Saturday morning either until after *The Lone Ranger* goes off," Paul said, sitting up in his bunk with this important bit of news.

Sean's laugh broke the surface, but he smothered it with a cough as he pushed Paul back down.

"Their bed is real big, Blair," Mandy said conversationally.

"Is it?" she asked on a high note. She gave folding back the counterpane an inordinate amount of attention.

"Sean's got one just as big, don't you, Sean? I've seen it," Andrew said.

"Have you ever seen Sean's bed?" Angela asked Blair.

"N . . . no. Good night now."

"Do you have a big bed like Sean's?" Mandy asked.

"No, stupid," Andrew said. "Didn't you see that sofa she has to sleep on?"

Mandy's face clouded with commiseration. "Maybe if you asked Sean he'd let you sleep with him in his big bed. He doesn't live very far from you."

"Our daddy doesn't mind Mommy sleeping with him," Angela added.

Blair's cheeks flamed scarlet and she didn't remember once in her life blushing before.

"Okay, that's all," Sean said with an intimidating voice. "Good night." He made certain all four pairs of eyes were closed before he turned to leave. After a cursory glance to the sleeping baby, who blessedly hadn't been able to contribute to the conversation, Blair joined him in the hallway. She tried to go past him, but he blocked her path.

"Do you have any favors to ask me?" he asked, his blue eyes dancing.

"No." She could still feel deep stains on her cheeks.

He laughed devilishly. Placing his hand on the back of her neck he said, "Let's go get something to eat."

Pam's dinner, for all her distractions while preparing it, was wonderful, as were Joe's steaks. The guests heaped their plates high from the buffet line and then selected places to sit either in the living room or on the patio.

Blair noticed that she and Sean were the object of many covert, speculative looks. He wasn't openly affectionate, but he was never far from her side either. He joined in the conversations around them, yet was constantly murmuring private asides into her ear. When she was talking to someone else, she felt his eyes on her, ever watchful.

Since he had fetched and carried for her throughout the meal, she insisted on carrying their plates into the kitchen when they were done. She scraped the refuse into the large plastic garbage can standing in the corner and took the plates to the sink to rinse them. She was just drying her hands on a paper towel when one of the guests came in behind her.

"That was quite a feed," he said, rubbing his hands over a potbelly.

He reminded her of "the toucher type," one of those annoying men who didn't think he could carry on a conversation with a woman unless he was pawing her. Men like that had always infuriated Blair. What made such men think she wanted or liked their clammy hands on her? From the moment she'd been introduced to him, she'd avoided him. He had said, "I could have guessed you were a dancer with legs like those." He had considered his remark amusing. She had thought it, like him, repugnant.

"Yes, it was a delicious meal."

He had deliberately placed himself between her and the door. "Get into the city often?"

"I just moved here a few days ago, Mr. . . ."

"Stan Collier. Call me Stan. All my friends do," he said in an oily voice.

"I haven't had an occasion to return to the city."

"Me, I have to commute every day on the damned train. Of course sometimes if business keeps me in the city for a dinner appointment, I stay over in the company's apartment. It's a nice little place. Private."

Blair couldn't believe this. If he weren't so disgusting, he'd be pitiful. Whatever was he doing as a guest of the Delgados? Surely Pam and Joe didn't condone this sleaziness.

"I'm sure it's very nice. Now if you'll excuse—"

"Anyway what I was thinking was maybe if you came into the city and found yourself free for lunch, you could—"

"Sell it somewhere else, Collier. Miss Simpson isn't interested." The hefty Stan whirled around with amazing agility when Sean's words rasped threateningly through the room. Blair sank against the countertop in relief. She hadn't been afraid of this overweight buffoon, she'd only been reluctant to cause a scene at Pam's party.

"Hey, Garrett, relax, relax," Stan Collier said with false bravado. His beefy forehead was perspiring profusely. "I was only funning with her. Can't you take a joke?"

"Yeah, I can take a joke," Sean said, with not the least hint of a smile on his rigid face. "I didn't hear anything funny. Blair?" He extended his hand and she rushed to it, grasping it like it was a safety rope. Sean enfolded her against him, more for the benefit of their observer than for her. Nonetheless, she pressed against him, welcoming the feeling of security his strong body lent hers.

They moved out of the room. "I hope you wanted to be rescued. Maybe you find Stan appealing," he murmured in her ear as his blond head bent over her.

"Oh, please," she said, shivering against him. "Do Pam and Joe know about him?"

"Everyone in Tidelands knows about him and his philandering. Or at least his claims to philandering. I'm not sure the exploits he brags about are more than wishful thinking."

"Why would Pam and Joe invite him here?"

"His wife is a darling woman. Everyone adores her and tolerates Stan because of her. He didn't single you out. He's made that same trite pass to everyone who wears a skirt."

"And here I thought I was special," she said with an exaggerated pout.

He laughed, then became serious as he stared down at her. "You are, but I doubt if anyone with Stan's indiscriminate taste would recognize just how special." He leaned closer and brushed the tip of his index finger over the tiny pearl in her ear. "I'm very discriminating."

She couldn't speak. The muscles of her throat closed around her vocal cords. The quipping reply she knew she should come back with was prohibited from ever being uttered. Instead she stood mute, losing herself in the depths of his blue eyes.

"Would you like some coffee?" Had he said, "Would you like to make love?" it couldn't have sounded more like an invitation to intimacy.

Tell him you can get your own coffee, Blair, her mind screamed. Instead her lips formed the words, "Yes, please. No sugar, a drop of cream." He backed away slowly, his eyes still charting her face.

Dazed, Blair drifted to a chair and sat down. She pretended to listen when one of the ladies started in on how deplorable the dance school in town was, but her mind was in a turmoil. Her heart failed to slow down even though she willed it to. The roaring in her ears drowned out the woman's tirade. Sean had kept his word. He hadn't made one move toward her that could be criticized and that wasn't in keeping with their agreement that they be friends only.

Why then her kamikaze gravitation toward him?

She didn't want to admit how nice it was to be looked after, to be fawned over. Always independent, she now reveled in relinquishing control to his masculine protectiveness. Had someone like Stan approached her months ago, she would have brushed him aside with a lashing insult that would have shocked him speechless and left his ears blistered and his ego crushed. She didn't want to concede how wonderful it had been to let Sean fight that battle for her. Just as seductive as his kisses, was the pleasure she found in being harbored by his virile strength.

"That's a terrific idea," Pam exclaimed, jolting Blair out of her reverie. "What do you think, Blair?"

"Uh, I . . ." she stuttered. Taking the saucer Sean was offering her, she realized that she had been the focal point of the unheard conversation going on around her. "I don't know," she said lamely. *What had they been talking about?*

Pam enlightened her. "The dance school here is terrible. I've wanted to get Mandy started on ballet, but didn't think I'd get my money's worth. And as you know if a child isn't taught properly from the first, there can be irreparable damage done to her muscles. Do you think you'd like to teach some classes while you're here?"

"Well—"

"I know I would love to take ballet," one of the ladies chimed in. "Nothing strenuous you understand, just stretching exercises to shave off some lumps." Several others concurred enthusiastically.

"You want *me* to teach ballet classes?" Blair asked, finally grasping the drift of the conversation.

"Yes! Why not?"

Chapter 5

Blair stared back at the expectant faces surrounding her and laughed uncomfortably. "Well for one thing, I'm not a teacher."

"But you're a dancer. The best I've ever seen. Now don't be modest," Pam rushed on when she saw Blair was about to object. "You love to dance and since you can't professionally for awhile, this might be the next best thing." The others nodded in agreement.

"Would it hurt your legs?" Blair turned to the quiet, low voice speaking close to her ear and looked into Sean's penetrating eyes.

"I don't think so. The doctor said that a minimum of regular exercise would be good for them and help them retain their strength. That way the climb back after six months' inactivity won't be so difficult."

"Then it's all set!" Pam said, her happy face beaming.

"Wait, wait, Pam. One has to have a studio, you know."

Pam's brow wrinkled in consternation. "Oh, yeah."

"You need a wooden floor, a large room?" Sean inquired.

Blair turned back to Sean. "Yes."

"I bought an old school gymnasium several months ago with the idea of one day converting it into a health club. It has such a room. You could use that. I'll do whatever reconstruction needs to be done."

"Terrific!" Pam clapped her hands.

"But I don't want to go into business," Blair protested. She felt she was being carried along by a current she couldn't fight.

"I won't charge you rent for the building and you won't charge your students. We'll consider it a community project." Sean silently polled the crowd and saw that everyone agreed.

"But I'll need records and something to play them on and . . ."

"I bought a record player at a police auction last month. I'll donate that," Joe said.

"Between us, you and I have got dance records

galore," Pam added. "So you see, Blair, you've got no problems."

She gnawed her bottom lip in contemplation. If living here less than a week had taught her one thing it was that time didn't move as fast in Tidelands as it did in the city. She was going to be here for six long months. If she didn't do something, she'd likely go mad. Was this the answer?

"I could teach basic ballet to students no older than twelve," she said slowly. "For you women I suppose I could conduct exercise classes, but I won't be able to do any strenuous calisthenics."

"We could do those on our own," one of the women contributed.

Pam took both of Blair's hands. "Then you'll say yes? Please, Blair. It'll be good for you, too. If I didn't think so, I wouldn't have suggested it."

Blair's eyes swept up to Sean. He was staring at her in that stirring way, but he neither encouraged nor discouraged her compliance. She looked back at Pam, shrugged, and said, "As you said, why not?"

All the guests had departed except Sean and Blair, who insisted on helping Pam clean up the mess left behind. "Do you do windows?" Pam asked facetiously as Blair stacked the last of the dishes into the dishwasher.

"Only when I can no longer see out them," she said, latching the door and starting the machine that wheezed as though in the throes of dying. "Will this thing make it through the cycle?" Blair asked.

"God, I hope so. Surely it wouldn't go out on me tonight. It couldn't be that cruel. By the way, did I ever thank you and Sean for getting those little heathens of mine to bed?"

"It was our pleasure," Sean said, coming in through the patio door where he and Joe had been enjoying one last cup of coffee. Sean winked at Blair and she struggled to hold back a giggle.

Their amusement was lost on Pam who went to Joe and collapsed into his waiting arms. "Great party, Hon," he said, hugging her tight. "You did yourself proud."

"Thanks, but I'm pooped."

"Then we'll say good night," Sean said, taking Blair's hand and leading her through the living room to the front door.

"I didn't mean to force you out," Pam said as she and Joe followed them to the door.

"I think Blair's had it, too. And now she's got a lot to think about."

"Did I really agree to start teaching ballet classes to kids and housewives?" she asked dismally.

"You sure did," Pam said cheerfully.

"As long as you understand that it's only temporary. Only for as long as I'm here."

Pam's smile drooped. "I'm not going to think about that. I've already become accustomed to your being in town."

All were quiet for a moment, then Sean said,

"She'll be here for six months at least. I don't let tenants out of their leases easily." They laughed then, grateful to him for relieving the momentary tension.

"If I can squeeze my fat body into an old leotard, I'll be the first one there when you start the exercise classes," Pam said.

"Don't work off too much flesh. I've grown so fond of it," Joe said from behind her, as he hugged his wife and nuzzled her neck.

"I think that's our cue," Sean said dryly.

"Good night and thank you for the party," Blair said as Sean steered her away from the door.

"Good night," Pam and Joe called in unison.

"Joe, I need to talk to you about what kind of roofing you want, but as tomorrow's Saturday, I won't call in the morning until after *The Lone Ranger*," Sean teased.

They heard Pam's soft, surprised gasp and Joe's hearty laugh before he closed the door.

Sean and Blair were still laughing when he pulled the Mercedes to a smooth stop in his driveway.

"Coffee? Nightcap?" he asked as he cut the motor.

"No. What you said is true. I've got a million things on my mind. Routines to work out, music to choose." She sighed dramatically. "What have I *done*?"

He chuckled as he opened his door and came around to open hers. No sooner had she stepped onto the ground than she was lifted into his arms. "We've got to take care of these knees now more than ever," he said. "You may be the last great hope for the women of Tidelands on the brink of obesity."

He had taken off his jacket early in the evening and rolled up his shirt sleeves. His arm was like a bar of iron that had been infused with life and warmth as it supported her back. To ward off the desire she felt unfurling inside her she asked, "Do you think anybody will really be interested in coming to the classes?"

"I'm sure they will. They all aspire to look like you. Impossible, of course, but you give them hope." At the top step, he ducked his head briefly to drop a chaste kiss on her forehead. "Good night, friend. Thank you for going to the party with me. I had a wonderful time."

He swung her down, but his kiss, brief and impersonal as it was, had weakened her to the point that she wasn't prepared to support herself. She landed on her knee the wrong way and she felt the abused tendons give way.

"Oh," she cried out when the pain stabbed under her kneecap like a knife.

"What? Oh, my God, what happened, Blair?" Sean fell to his own knees to better inspect hers as she leaned over and massaged the injured joint.

"It's . . . it's nothing," she said unsteadily, trying to block out the wave of dizziness that accompanied the pain. "I landed wrong, that's all. Hurts like hell."

"God, I'm sorry," he said in an anguished voice

before raising her skirt to place his hands around her knee.

"It's not your fault, Sean. It happens all the time. At least this time I was in front of my own door. Last time it gave out, I was shopping in Bloomingdale's on a Saturday no less."

She tried to laugh away his anxiety and her pain, but his face was grim as he stood, propping her against him, and opened the door. He lifted her again and carried her into the darkened apartment, depositing her in a chair. "Sean—"

"Stay right there," he instructed as he left her to switch on the lamp on the end table. "Do you have any medication to take for that?"

She shook her head. "I didn't have the prescription for pain pills filled. I didn't want to get started on anything like that."

"Aspirin?"

"Yes, I'd take a couple of aspirins."

"Where are they?" He had pulled down the sofa and converted it into her bed. There was something disturbingly personal about his handling the linens she had slept on the night before.

"In the bathroom. The cabinet over the sink. But really—"

She was speaking to his shadow as he disappeared into the bathroom. She heard him fumbling in the tiny cabinet, a soft curse, the water running. Then he was back with a glass of water and two aspirins looking like dots in his massive palm.

"Should you rub something on it? An ointment or something?"

She swallowed the aspirins. "No. I'll just elevate it while I'm sleeping. Don't worry about it. By morning it'll be fine."

"What happened?" He knelt in front of her and, before she could stop him, was working at the thin laces wrapped around her ankles and taking off the gold sandals.

"One of those tendons or ligaments or whatever twisted when I came down on it. They're weak and can't take some forms of stress."

He looked up at her from his kneeling position. "Do you have to go to the bathroom before I tuck you in for the night?"

She was struck dumb by the question, then realized how ridiculous that sentiment was. "Uh, I'd probably better," she answered, not quite meeting his eyes.

He scooped her in his arms again and carried her to the door. When he set her down, he made sure she was supporting herself with her better leg. "Hop the rest of the way."

"You're over-reacting."

"Someone has to treat these injuries sensibly, for it's sure as hell you don't."

She glared at him and then shut the door in his face. "Hop!" he called through it.

When she was finished, he was waiting for her on the other side of the door, not having budged from his post. "What do you sleep in?"

"Sean," she said gratingly.

"Okay, if you'd rather sleep in the buff, that's—"

"There are some T-shirts in the top drawer of the bureau," she said with resignation. He was bent on carrying out the Clara Barton routine and she really had no choice but to play along.

He came back carrying a T-shirt with *42nd Street* printed on it.

"Were you in this show?"

"Yes. Did you see it?"

"Yes."

"Then surely you remember me. I was the one in the tap shoes."

"Very funny," he said.

This bantering conversation was designed to distract them from the moment of truth that had just come upon them. She had to get out of her dress.

"Does this go up or down?" he asked in a husky voice.

"I can manage."

"Up or down?" The determination that made his eyes go as hard and incisive as diamonds was unconquerable. She couldn't conjure up enough will to try.

"Down," she whispered, dropping her eyes to stare at the floor.

The bowed position of her head aided him in unfastening the buttons behind her neck holding up her halter. When they were released, he gradually lowered the bodice. She saw his hands moving restlessly, indecisively, as they adjusted the material around her waist.

"There's a button here," Blair mumbled. In what she thought would be an impatient gesture, she fumbled past his hands to find the button at her waist. But by groping through the fabric in her search, the backs of her hands bumped against his in what evolved into a caress. His hands were lifted by the movements of hers, lifted until the tips of his fingers were scarce inches from her breasts. Both regretted when the button was found and undone.

The dress fell to the floor around her feet and she stood before him wearing only the scantiest of panties.

"I'll get it later," Sean said about the dress. His breath was warm against her face, her neck, her chest. So warm. He gathered the T-shirt in his hands and pulled it over her head, helping her poke her arms through the sleeves. He pulled it down to barely cover the band of her panties. "There." He sounded relieved.

He picked her up again and carried her to the bed, lowering her onto it with the care of a mother for her new infant. He turned away quickly as she scrambled to cover herself with the sheet.

"Does this go in the closet?" he asked, keeping his back to her as he picked up the dress.

"Yes. Thank you," she said softly, momentarily closing her eyes against the desire to see him lying down beside her.

He carefully arranged the dress on a hanger and hung it in the closet. "Would you like anything else? Some tea? Wine?"

She shook her head. The hair she had just released from its restricting pins swayed over her shoulders. "No. I'm fine."

He sat down on the edge of the mattress and looked at her for long silent moments. Had he taken her in his arms then, she admitted later that she wouldn't have resisted. She wanted nothing more than to feel the touch of his lips against hers, hard and persistent, banishing her caution. She wanted his soothing hands on her body, coaxing her into responses she knew lay just below the surface of her skin, responses too long denied and dying for the chance to live. She wanted to hear him pouring words into her ear, bold, stimulating love words she'd never allowed any other man to say. Whether he meant them or not, she longed to hear them coming from his beautiful mouth, filtering through that sensuous mustache.

But he didn't take her in his arms. Rather he asked softly, "Don't you need a pillow under that knee?"

"Yes, probably."

He retrieved the second pillow, the one that wasn't blessed with her curtain of dark hair fanning over it, and lifted the sheet. His teeth clamped together to prevent him from groaning at the sight of her naked legs between the smooth sheets. Her breasts lay flat against her chest, with only the pouting of her nipples to inflame him. Her stomach was concave beneath her rib cage and the inch of skin between the hem of her T-shirt and the lacy top of her panties beckoned to him seductively.

Striving for objectivity, he adjusted the pillow under her knee and gently bent it over the cushiony support. He couldn't resist sliding his hand down her shin and then around it to cup the firm muscle of her calf. Her eyes refused to remain open and she sighed as her lashes settled on her cheek.

When next she felt his touch, his finger was gliding over that velvety ribbon of skin on her abdomen that had so intrigued him. "Blair, please look at me."

Slowly she lifted the veil of dark lashes. The lamplight highlighted one side of his face, while the other was cast in deep shadow. The cleft in his chin looked deeper, more masculine and rugged than ever. His hair shone in the golden light.

"I want you," he said with deep intensity. "You know that. I haven't made a secret of it." The backs of his fingers celebrated the softness of her cheek. "When you realize what good friends we are," he smiled slightly, "I'm going to kiss you here." His index finger outlined her lips with a feathery touch that eventually floated down her neck to her chest. "And here." He caressed her nipple through the soft cotton of her shirt and was rewarded with a firm response. "Here," he said, massaging her navel hypnotically with his finger. He lowered his hand farther and touched her again. "Here," he said gruffly. "Everywhere."

Her back and neck arched reflexively and a small cry of helplessness escaped her lips. Her face was captured between his hands, and stroking thumbs adored the bone structure of her cheeks.

"Sean," she sighed.

"Good night." He leaned down to kiss her lightly on the lips, his mustache no more than a whisper against her mouth.

Hurriedly he snapped out the light, crossed the room and let himself out the door. Blair followed his footsteps until they faded into silence. She heard his back door close behind him.

She was left alone in the dark. Alone with the imprints of his fingers burning her skin wherever they had touched. Alone with her imagination branding erotic fantasies on her mind. Alone with that ever-widening chasm deep inside her that ached to be filled.

She was sipping her second cup of tea at the kitchen table and tentatively rotating her knee when she heard him coming up the stairs. He knocked softly.

"Come in," she called. She had put on a pair of shorts and an elasticized strapless tube-top as soon as she had gotten out of bed and tested the strength of her knee. Thankfully she could walk without any discomfort.

He opened the door she had unlocked earlier and came in, his face scowling. "What are you doing out of bed?"

"Drinking tea," she retorted, stating the obvious.

"Smart aleck. Doesn't your knee hurt?"

"I could be cute and say something like, 'Only when I laugh,' or 'Only when I breathe,' but I'd never stoop to such banality."

"Then it does hurt."

She laughed at the deep line of concern that furrowed between his brows. "Will you relax? No, it doesn't hurt. I don't think it's up to a performance of *A Chorus Line* or running the Boston marathon, but I can walk. Would you like some tea?"

"I despise tea."

"Really? I thought all Irishmen loved their tea. How about one chorus of 'Danny Boy'?" she taunted.

"You must be feeling better. You've regained your glib tongue. If you weren't already battered, I'd be tempted to punish your insolence."

"How? By giving me a well-deserved spanking?"

His eyes ran up and down the length of her body, taking in the tightly stretched knit over her breasts. "There are other, more pleasant means of discipline." He didn't need to resort to physical demonstration. Just the suggestion of it and the underlying tension in his voice had caused the tongue he had termed glib to stick to the roof of her mouth. "I came by this morning to see if you wanted to go look at your new studio."

Blair hoped that her act had been played well. Her flippant remarks had been a defense against the fluttering of her heart and the profusion of perspiration that had bathed her palms when she'd heard his footsteps coming up the stairs. Her dreams had revolved around him. All night she had been haunted by memories of past kisses and tormented by fantasies of kisses yet to come.

Repeatedly she had assured herself that her sleeplessness was due to her aching knee and the uncomfortable position of lying on her back, but by dawn she still wasn't convinced. She only hoped that the faint purple circles under her eyes had been successfully covered by make-up.

It frightened her, this preoccupation with a man she barely knew. Things were happening too quickly and she couldn't seem to get a grip on the reins of her own life. When they had slipped through her fingers, she didn't recall, but she thought it was about the time she had opened the door to a masseur and saw Sean Garrett.

She realized, too, that there was no halfway point on which they could meet. They could never be just friends, and saying that they could was only game playing. They both knew that. He had confessed without any apology his desire to become her lover. Toward that culmination, she seemed to fly, knowing all the while it was impossible for her to become involved with any man, especially one she had absolutely nothing in common with.

The only thing to do was to refrain from seeing too much of him. Out of sight, out of mind. Put the temptation off limits—that had been her resolution as she dragged herself from her bed this morning. Now it was being put to the test.

"I can drive myself over if you give me directions. I'm sure you have other work to do." Leaving the table, she went to the sink to rinse out her cup. She didn't care if the cup were rinsed out or not, but it gave her a feasible excuse to turn her back on him. She found him too damned attractive. His jeans were too tight across his loins, his thighs and sex too well defined. The polo shirt conformed to the tapering of his waist from the broad sculptured curves of his shoulders and upper chest.

"Today's Saturday. I usually don't work on Saturday."

"Well then you wouldn't want to take me over there because that would be work for you. I'll go by myself either today or tomorrow."

"But you won't be able to get into the building because . . ." He fished in the front pocket of his jeans, something she wished he wouldn't do because it stretched the cotton even tighter across his masculinity. "Because I have the only key."

Her relief that he had accomplished his task was exchanged for irritation. He was dangling the single key on the brass ring inches in front of her eyes. "I guess it's too much to hope for that you would simply turn the key over to me."

His mustache drooped in parody of a sympathetic expression. "I'm sorry." His sparkling eyes said otherwise.

"Um-huh. I'm sure you're just eaten up with grief."

His mustache then spread wide over a huge white smile. "Come on. Let's go. Have you had breakfast? How about picking up a dozen donuts on the way?"

"Donuts!" she exclaimed. "If I eat breakfast at all, I have a carton of plain yogurt."

He shrugged. "I can tell that enticing you off the straight and narrow into a life of sin and corruption is going to take some work. Come on."

Barely giving her time to grab her purse, he hauled her out of the apartment, carried her down the stairs and put her in the front seat of his ancient pickup truck.

"You don't have to try to impress me," she said sarcastically as she critically eyed the cracked vinyl upholstery with tufts of cotton sprouting from it like blossoms. The bare metal floor was littered with blueprints long used and forgotten and a variety of tools, some of which Blair couldn't identify.

Sean only grinned as he ground the truck into gear and it chugged out of the driveway. "Love me, love my truck."

Negating her protests, he stopped at a bakery to purchase a sack full of donuts. He stowed it on the seat between them, and Blair's stomach growled when the yeasty aroma filled the cab of the truck. Sean roared with laughter. He stopped at a convenience store and bought a quart of milk, then they bounced through the streets in the derelict truck to the vacant building he was donating for her use as a studio.

Leaving their breakfast for later, he came around to lift her down from the truck and carry her to the door of the building. "This isn't necessary, Sean," she said as he followed the sidewalk rather than taking the well-worn path across the dried grass.

"That's debatable since I saw the pain on your face last night, but in any event it allows me to get my hands on you."

She hadn't wanted to admit how she had looked forward to being held in his arms. She loved the feel of his hard chest against her side. Her arms had quite naturally encircled his neck to lock just beneath the strands of hair that brushed his collar. The touch of his bare arm under her bare legs sent electric currents through her body. The hand belonging to the arm that supported her back folded around her side to lightly touch her breast with his fingertips.

"Besides, what's a little familiarity between good friends?" he whispered in her ear.

She immediately lowered her arms and was annoyed when he only laughed. He set her down gently, making sure her leg wasn't going to give way as it had done the night before. He inserted the key in the lock and said by way of warning, "It doesn't look like much, so don't panic. Give me a week or so and I'll have it in tip-top shape."

He was right to warn her. Otherwise her gasp of horror might have been even louder than it was. The place was a disaster. The floor could barely be seen because of the discarded lumber and debris that obscured it. Great chunks of plaster had fallen from the ceiling. The walls were scarred and gouged for reasons Blair could only guess at. The whole room looked as if it had been pillaged by an enraged giant and left to give testimony of his temper.

She turned to look up at Sean helplessly, dismay written on every feature, her green eyes clouded with bewilderment. He placed a reassuring arm around her shoulder. "Chin up. I told you not to panic."

"But this . . . this is impossible."

"Never say impossible. You should see some of the 'before' pictures of houses I've restored. They've had a century or better to deteriorate. This building has only had about forty years." He laughed at her stupefaction. "First thing Monday morning, I'll get a wrecking crew to haul off everything that isn't nailed down. A wall man will come in and do those repairs, a ceiling man will do that, etc. Do the floors look okay?"

He shoved a pile of wormy lumber aside to let her see the floor beneath. She knelt down. "Yes, I think so."

"Someone will sand and revarnish it. The skylight looks intact and weatherproof, but I'll check it."

Now that the initial shock had worn off, she began to recognize a few of the room's merits. She gazed up at the skylight that ran the length of the room. "I like that," she said. "There's nothing worse than a dreary studio."

"What will you need, Blair? I confess to total ignorance as to what a dance studio should look like."

"One wall will need to be mirrored." As she talked, he took mental notes. "A *barre* of course. I think I can give you possibilities of where to find these types of things in the city."

"Okay. What else?"

"I guess there should be some sort of dressing room."

"There's a large one in the back with toilets and showers. I'll see that they're renovated and in working order. There's also a small office you can use. You may want to lock up your record player, records, and whatever else you use in there. I'll fix it up."

"Sean," she said worriedly. "I hate for you to go to any expense on this. And I know it's going to cost you a lot of money. I think I should tell Pam that this isn't going to work. You—"

"Let me worry about the expense. I volunteered the building. It's not doing anyone any good just sitting here rotting. It's an eye sore. It might just as well be a studio for dance classes."

"But it's so temporary," she cried.

"Is it?" His eyes seemed to blaze into her brain.

For a moment she was stunned into silence by his piercing gaze. "Yes. As soon as I can, I'm resuming my career in the city," she said adamantly.

"Then you shouldn't be concerned about what I do in the meantime," he said coldly. "I told you last night I bought this building with the intention of one day converting it into a health club. This will be only the first renovation. I consider it an investment."

Stung by his biting words and hostile attitude, she turned away from him and picked her way through the rubbish on the floor. She had to put distance between them. Space. Air. She couldn't think clearly around him. For a heartbeat, when he had prodded her, she had been uncertain that returning to her work was what she wanted. *Of course it was!* That's all she lived for. But the incident only pointed up to her how his sensuality jeopardized her sound judgment.

The more she explored the room, the more impossible seemed the task to convert it into anything, much less a place in which to teach dance. Sean went on his own expedition, thumping the walls periodically to find beams and locate hollow places.

Blair reached the door to the small office Sean had mentioned and after some hard shoving, it swung open. She had peered through the dusty glass on the top part of the door to see that the room was as littered and filthy as the rest of the building, so she wasn't surprised by the musty smell that assailed her nostrils.

What she didn't expect was the scurrying family of mice that scattered in every direction when the opening door roused them. Only Blair's piercing scream prevented one from running over her sandaled feet. She went on screaming as the terrified mouse changed direction, his tail whipping behind him, to streak under the army green metal filing cabinet in the corner.

"Blair?" Sean shouted in alarm and came hurdling over the piles of debris toward her.

She, in turn, fairly flew over the unsteady floor,

heedless of the danger she was courting for her injuries.

"Be careful, Blair," Sean cautioned. "Don't— Wait—"

She vaulted into his chest, arms clasping around his neck, legs wrapping around his waist as he caught her to him. She buried her face in his throat. Hurriedly he carried her to the less littered place near the door. He stroked her hair with one hand while supporting her bottom with the other. She was trembling. Her breath hiccuped against the skin of his throat.

"Shhhh. It's okay. I've got you." He murmured into her hair, holding her tight. "What was it? Snake? Spider? Rat?"

She raised a chalky face toward his. Her green eyes were wide with horror. "Rats? God. I thought they were mice. Rats?" She shuddered and, squeezing her eyes shut, lay her face against the strong column of his neck again.

"It may have been only mice and I'll bet they were as frightened of you as you were of them."

She shook her head. "I hate things like that. Little things with beady eyes that scurry furtively. Why anyone would ever want a white rat or a gerbil or anything like that for a pet has always been beyond my comprehension."

"I promise never to give you anything smaller than a St. Bernard for a gift."

She realized then that he was speaking directly into her ear. That his mouth had pushed aside her hair and was leaving a damp vapor on her skin. His mustache was caressing the side of her neck and his teeth were gently scraping her skin.

She lifted her head and pushed away from him as far as she could. "I feel like a fool, acting the way I did, flying at you like that."

"I assure you I didn't mind." His eyes were glinting with teasing lights and his mouth was tilted into a self-satisfied smile.

Blair then became painfully aware of their position. His hands were cupped under her hips as he held her against him. Her ankles were locked behind his back at his waist. She blushed hotly at the implicit juxtaposition of their bodies.

"I . . . I'm fine now. You can let me down."

"It's no trouble. Really," he said sincerely.

"Sean," she said threateningly and he laughed.

"At least let me get you out of here." He carried her that way until they had passed through the door. She tried to avoid his eyes that stared directly into hers. He was enjoying every movement, every jostle, every brush of his body against hers. Once through the door, he regretfully lowered her to the concrete and turned to relock the door. By the time he was finished, she was halfway to the truck.

"I'm supposed to carry you," he called to her.

"I've told you, I'm fine. If I don't exercise these legs, they'll get stiff."

She thought she heard him mumble a vicious curse, but she pulled herself up into the cab of the truck and slammed the screeching door behind her. If he had touched her again she would have exploded and disintegrated, never to be restored to Blair Simpson again. The fragments of her might be assembled into someone else, but if she let him touch her once more the way every cell in her body was clamoring to be touched, she would never belong to herself again. She would be lost.

He started the truck and said conversationally, "Don't worry about the restoration. In a few days, you won't recognize the place."

"I hope not," she said grouchily. How could he be so casual when she was quaking on the inside? Was he accustomed to holding women in his arms, to having them melt against him with no regard to propriety, morality, or decency? Did he go blithely on his way after each embrace as though nothing had happened?

"And the first thing I'll do is set some traps so it will be completely mouse free."

"Thanks," she said curtly.

"Still hungry or did fright take away your appetite as well as your good humor?" he asked, swinging the pickup into the lane leading to the township's small municipal park. She ignored his jibe, sitting stonily at his side as he pulled under the sprawling branches of an oak and cut the choking motor of the truck. "Breakfast is served, Madam," he said in the somber deadpan tones of a stuffy butler.

"Go to hell," she said, but already the corners of her mouth were twitching with the need to laugh.

"Tsk, tsk, no earthy language. I may stop respecting you. And if I ever stop respecting you, look out."

His index finger trailed her inner thigh upward from her knee. She caught his hand just before it reached the leg of her shorts.

She wished her voice held more conviction and wasn't shaking so when she said, "Well, I've never respected you."

She had to put her shoulder to the door before it would open and then she nearly fell out of the truck in a headlong plunge when it came free. He was still laughing when he joined her at the picnic table, bringing the carton of milk and the sack of donuts with him. "That was a graceful step. What do you do for an encore?"

She sputtered searching for a comeback, was chagrined to find that she couldn't form one, and joined in his laughter as she climbed onto the redwood table. He dug into the sack and produced a glazed donut. "For you." When he saw she was about to decline, he glared at her menacingly.

"Maybe just half," she conceded.

"No, no. We've got Bavarian cream filled and chocolate covered when we get through with these," he said, closing his strong white teeth on half of his donut.

She managed to eat two, licking her fingers of the Bavarian cream much to his delight. When they were done, he tossed the crumbs onto the ground. "You don't have an aversion to birds, do you? They have beady eyes."

"But they don't scurry."

"That's true," he said, smiling and brushing his

hands free of crumbs. They watched as a flock of sparrows greedily attacked that unexpected treat. "Ready for some milk?" he asked, opening the carton.

"Just a sip. Do we have cups?"

"Cups!?" he asked in feigned mortification. "What's the fun of eating outside if you use conventional symbols of civilization like cups?" He handed her the carton.

She eyed the V-shaped spout warily. "I don't think this fits my mouth, but here goes." She swallowed a mouthful before she felt twin rivers of milk dribbling down each corner of her mouth to her chin. Lowering the carton, she laughed, trying to wipe up the dripping milk with her hands.

Her wrists were manacled by strong fingers. He hopped off the table to stand in front of her. "Allow me." He watched entranced as the two rivulets of milk funneled into one and rolled down her chest to form a creamy drop on the top curve of her breasts.

He stared at the drop for a long time before he lowered his head and lifted it from her skin with his tongue. He heard her short, soft huff of pleasure and smiled against the skin under his lips. Leisurely, he kissed away all remnants of the milk, using his tongue to bathe away any residue. He worked his way up her chest to her neck, taking an excessive amount of time, devoting far more skill to the chore than it warranted.

Reaching her mouth after long minutes, he licked at her lips lightly with his tongue, torturing her by not doing more. When he pulled back slightly he heard her moan of protest. "All clean," he said, barely making a sound with the words.

Blair felt suspended by tenuous threads over a vat of boiling desire. One by one she had felt those threads snap as Sean's mouth had tantalized each feminine instinct in her body and brought her senses to acute attention. Now she felt it was predestined that she fall into that roiling abyss and be absorbed by it.

"Not quite all," she whispered and leaned forward. One crystal of a donut's sugary glaze was clinging to his mustache. It dissolved against the tip of her tongue. Emboldened by her own daring, she raked her tongue along the underside of his mustache, teasing his upper lip with darting flicks.

The fingers around her wrists flexed and his chest pressed against hers as he moved forward. His voice was serrated as he growled, "Miss Simpson, unless you have a penchant for making love on public picnic tables, I suggest you cease and desist immediately."

Her head snapped up sharply. He winked at her, kissed her surprised mouth soundly and smackingly, and then said, "Besides, we have a lot of work to do."

Chapter 6

They both did have a lot of work to do and the next week sped by. Sean divided his time between the house he was currently working on, the addition to the Delgados' house, and the dance studio. He had contracted specialists in each field to do the work required, but in the afternoons he checked on them to make sure they did everything according to his high standards. When Blair wasn't able to accompany him, he reported the progress to her.

These progress reports were usually given over dinner either at his house or in her apartment or in one of the fine restaurants lining the beach. If Blair felt uneasy about the vast amount of time they were spending in each other's company, she justified it by telling herself it was for the sake of business.

One evening Pam and Joe showed up on her doorstep toting the promised record player. "We thought you might need a few days to get used to operating it," Joe said, carrying it in and setting it on the kitchen table.

"Where are the children?" Blair asked.

"At home with Andrew in charge. He rules like a despot when we're not around, so we need to get back before he's assassinated. Mandy has signed up for your Monday-Wednesday class."

"I think every little girl in town has," Blair said. She went on to tell them how her phone had not stopped ringing since an ad had been placed in the local newspaper. Word of mouth was as responsible as anything for the publicity the dance classes were receiving. "The ladies exercise class is also filling up. I'm going to have to limit the number of registrants or there won't be room to move."

"I knew this idea was inspired," Pam said. "Only three more days and you start. Will the building be finished?"

"Sean swears it will. It's shaping up far better than I dared hope."

"No one but Sean could have pulled it off on such short notice. He's a slave driver, but the men who work for him would march into a wall of fire if he asked them to," Joe said.

"You look fit enough," Pam said, surveying Blair. "How are your knees holding up?"

"Stronger each day." She had been exercising cautiously in the mornings and resting her legs each afternoon by treating them to warm baths and keeping them elevated for several hours. "Do you still want to help me work out those calisthenic routines? If I show you the steps, can you lead the class?"

"I can't wait to get on my dancing shoes again!"

Just then Sean threw open the door and stuck his head inside. "I only have two cheeseburgers, two orders of fries, two malteds—one chocolate and one vanilla, but we're willing to share. *Aren't* we?" he asked Blair mischievously.

She rushed to relieve him of the take-out food and he shook hands with Joe. "We're just leaving and Pam left a pot roast in the oven."

"Pot roast," Sean said, licking his lips.

"I'll trade you one pot roast meal with five children for one cheeseburger eaten in peace," Pam offered. Sean and Blair declined graciously. "Can't say that I blame you."

The Delgados took their leave shortly, but not before Pam winked at Blair conspiratorially. There was no doubt in Blair's mind the message that wink conveyed. She knew she and Sean were raising eyebrows all over town and romantic hearts were pattering with glee.

They would be disappointed if they knew the true state of affairs. Since their picnic breakfast, Sean hadn't touched her except when necessary out of politeness. He made no sexual innuendos, instigated no personal conversations, initiated no romantic scenes.

He treated her like a well-admired friend or a close business partner.

Each night as they parted company, he might or might not kiss her lightly on the cheek with the detachment of a fond relative, but there were no repetitions of the heart-stopping embraces they had shared before. Blair told herself she was glad he had finally heeded her wishes, but she wondered why she found it hard to concentrate on the simplest tasks; why she poured body and soul into her mild workouts as though trying to rid herself of a persistent parasite; why there was inside her a restlessness that couldn't quite be defined.

As promised, Sean had the studio ready in time for classes to open. The night before the big day, he took Blair for one last inspection tour. The mirrored wall reflected her astonished expression that he had brought about such a transformation. The floor had been sanded and treated as necessary for a dance studio; the *barre*, ordered from the city, had been positioned along the wall according to her specifications. The tile showers in the dressing room gleamed; the office was equipped with a small desk, a new filing cabinet, an easy chair, and a telephone.

"One hundred percent mouse free," Sean said as he opened the door to it.

She overcame her bafflement to say, "Sean, this is . . . is too much. I wanted something livable, but this is deluxe. I've never worked in a studio this nice in Manhattan."

"As I told you before it's an investment," he shrugged. "I'm only selfishly planning for the future."

She didn't believe him, but didn't argue with him either. If his goal had been to instill her with enthusiasm for her new project, he had succeeded. She couldn't wait until the next morning for her first class.

By the time the class was over, her enthusiastic outlook had drastically altered and she was almost ready to throw in the towel. She had had to cope with twenty-five excited little girls and twenty-five obnoxious mothers. "You gotta be kiddin'," she said to Pam as she collapsed into the comfortable chair in the office. Silently she thanked Sean for his foresight in installing a chair other than the one behind the desk.

Pam laughed as she stationed Mandy in front of her to rebraid her hair. "Wait until you get thirty-five overweight, out-of-shape housewives who want a body like yours within two or three weeks. They'll dance their pounding hearts out then go home to their secret cache of M&Ms." Pam struggled with the rubber band at the end of the plait. "What are you doing?"

"Making a sign," Blair said, sweeping one last flourish with the Magic Marker on a piece of white cardboard. Then she held her handiwork against her chest for Pam to read.

" 'Mothers are welcome the first class of each month. Otherwise please leave your child at the door. Thank you, Blair,' " Pam said. "You learn quick, kid."

Indeed she learned a lot within the next couple of weeks. She learned that grown women had to be reminded that they couldn't gossip and do strenuous exercises at the same time. She learned that children should never dance with bubble gum in their mouths lest they go home with it enmeshed in their hair. She learned how to mop up accidental puddles when little girls didn't give themselves enough time to run to the bathroom and grapple with leotards and tights. She learned that women can get hostile when told not to bring cups of coffee onto the dance floor please.

Yet each night over their dinner, which they had a silent agreement to share together, she recounted these events to Sean with her eyes shining brightly and her gestures animated. She didn't realize how happy she looked, how seldom she talked about her knees that gave her very little trouble if she were careful in demonstrating steps. When she fell into her sofa bed at night, she slept the sleep of the just, exhausted, but always eager to get up and face the challenges of the next day.

As she was locking the door after her last class late one Friday afternoon, Sean was waiting for her in his Mercedes parked at the curb. She waved to him as she walked conscientiously on the sidewalk and not the grass that, due to Sean's daily watering, was struggling for survival.

"Why are you so late?" he called out the car window. "Everyone left a long time ago."

Blair was sure everyone leaving had taken note that he was waiting for her, too. "I worked out a while and then showered."

"Do you like champagne?"

"Only when chilled to perfection," she yelled back.

"Then you're in luck. It's been on ice all day." He climbed out of his car, detoured her from the borrowed car she was still driving, and propelled her to the passenger side of his Mercedes. "Pam said she'd have Joe bring her by and drive the car back to your apartment. Tonight, we're celebrating with a picnic dinner on the beach."

"To what do I owe this dubious honor?"

"To the fact that you're reasonably sane after two weeks of dance classes with the ladies and girls of Tidelands," he teased, starting the motor and steering out of the parking lot. He had on shorts and a T-shirt. The setting sunlight caught on his legs and burnished the hair that dusted his skin.

"That does call for a celebration, but do you mind your date being dressed like this?" She had slipped on a clean leotard and wrapped a denim skirt around her waist when she'd finished her shower. Her hair was still damp, parted down the middle and left to dry naturally, which meant perfectly straight.

He scanned her out of the corner of his eye. "I guess you'll do." When she looked at him with murder in her eyes, he laughed. "You know I always think you look beautiful." Reaching across the interior of the car, he slipped his hand under her skirt and lay it on her knee. The shock that missiled through both of them went straight to their hearts. It was the first time in weeks that he'd touched her with anything but friendly companionship and it ignited all the pent-up tension and passion that both had been trying desperately to bank.

"How are your legs?" he asked softly.

"Fine," she said in a gravelly voice, then cleared her throat. "I talked to the doctor yesterday. He said to continue doing what I'm doing. He wants to see me in a month."

The fingers around her knee tensed briefly before regretfully sliding away. He pulled into the driveway of a house with a beach front. It was Victorian in design, with a surrounding veranda, cupolas in each corner of the front on the upper story, and filigreed woodwork outlining the porch covering.

"This is one of the houses I restored for a client. They own a stretch of the beach, but I've been given permission to use it when they're not here. I happen to know they're in Europe, so our privacy is guaranteed."

The intensity underlying his words made her heart skip several beats before starting again with a rapid, erratic tempo. The sunset was painting the entire atmosphere indigo. An ocean breeze cooled her cheeks as she opened the car door and stepped out.

"Not so fast," Sean said to her as she pushed open the gate leading onto the property. "I can't carry all this by myself."

"What in the world do you have?"

He took a blanket, a regulation picnic basket, and a Styrofoam cooler out of the backseat. "Can you carry the blanket and basket? This thing's heavy," he said in reference to the cooler.

"Styrofoam?"

"No," he said dryly. "The contents. Two bottles of champagne."

"Two?"

"Yes. I intend to ply you with drink and then take lascivious advantage of you."

She laughed lightly as she sashayed through the gate. They made their way around the house and took the path through tall grass to the beach. Sean spread the blanket and Blair collapsed on it, stretching her legs out in front of her. Situating their cargo within reach, they breathed deeply of the salty air.

"Ah, Mother Nature, there's nothing like her," Sean sighed. His appreciation for nature went even further. He whipped his T-shirt over his head and hopped on alternate feet until he rid himself of his running shoes. Then to Blair's utter dismay, he unsnapped his shorts and they dropped to his ankles rendering him—

Totally naked! She hadn't even the breath to gasp, to scold. Her breath had been suctioned out of her lungs at the sight of his beautiful manhood so nonchalantly displayed.

Paralyzed where she sat, she watched his hand extend down to her. "Join me?"

She shook her head, still dumbfounded. He didn't insist. Instead he turned and headed toward the surf. To his retreating back, she said asthmatically, "Not just now."

He walked into the sparkling water with the arrogant swagger of a nautical god. The lace-edged waves lapped at his ankles and calves as though bestowing on them kisses of worship. He executed a horizontal dive into a wave that embraced him like a lover. When next she saw him, his strong arms were arcing over the surface as he swam away from shore. Coming back, he relaxed and let the tide carry him in.

He stood up and cupped his hands over his mouth to call to her. "Come on in. It feels great."

She shook her head and found enough voice to yell back, "Too cold." Later, she would recall that she hadn't even looked at his face. Her eyes had riveted on the beguiling arrow of hair that pointed down his stomach to what lay just beneath the surface of the water. In the diminishing light that part of him was only revealed at the caprice of waves that sloshed against him with a rhythm deliberately timed to tease her.

When he came running out of the surf, she averted her head and murmured inconsequentially about the spectacular sunset. His breathing was rough from exertion, hers none the less so. But hers became easier as she saw out of her peripheral vision that he was stepping into his shorts. She exhaled gratefully when she heard the top fastener snapping closed.

"Whew," he said, rubbing his hands through his wet hair. "That was great. Now I'm hungry. How about you?"

Hungry? Her insides were churning, but not with the kind of hunger he was speaking of. Never, if she lived to be a thousand years old, would she forget how he looked with the last rays of the evening's sun tinting his body to a deep bronze, highlighting and shadowing in a way that would make artistic spirits soar. Clothed he was breathtaking. Naked he epitomized manhood in its most excellent form.

To cover her uneasiness, she asked cockily, "What's for supper?" She looked just past his shoulder, not quite ready to meet his perceptive blue eyes.

"Lobster salad, deviled eggs, French bread, assorted relishes, and strawberry tarts."

"This is a celebration! Don't tell me you prepared all of it."

"I wish I could take the credit, but no, I had the chef at The Lighthouse pack the basket for me." Taking the first bottle of champagne out of the cooler and scraping off the ice chips that clung to it, he said, "First things first."

Adroitly, he peeled away the foil, unloosed the wire, and popped the cork out of the bottle. The aromatic vapor from the fermenting champagne drifted out of the bottleneck, whetting their thirsts for a taste of the biting, crisp wine. Taking two stemmed glasses out of the basket, he poured each of them a generous amount before returning the bottle to the cooler.

He held his glass aloft and clinked it against hers. "To the most graceful, most beautiful, most . . . sexiest dancing teacher I've ever known."

Blair laughed, but acknowledged the compliments with a regal nod of her head. They both sipped and sighed in delight at the cold pleasure of the wine. Then leaning toward her, he settled his lips against hers. "Congratulations on a job well done."

"Thank you."

The kiss was devoid of passion, but rife with a tenderness that made Blair's breasts ache. Too soon for her, he ended it.

She helped him unload the basket and they attacked the delicious dishes like a pair of ravenous wolves. The first bottle of champagne was polished off within a matter of minutes. They were well into the second when Blair licked the last crumbs of strawberry tart from her fingers and fell back onto the blanket, her appetite fully satisfied.

"I'm going to burst," she said, rubbing her stomach.

"Good," Sean replied quietly. Storing the leftovers in the basket and setting it aside, he stretched out next to her.

She rolled her head to the side to look at him. "That was delicious. Thank you. It's wonderful here."

"You're wonderful," he said thickly. "You look wonderful. Sound wonderful. Taste wonderful." The inches between them lessened until his mouth fastened onto hers in a telling kiss. One appetite may have been satiated, but one was still a gnawing emptiness within them both.

He feasted on her mouth as though it were a delectable piece of fruit fashioned and created for him alone. Her fingers plowed through his wealth of silver-blond hair and held his mouth in place while she sampled it with the thoroughness of a connoisseur.

When they fell apart, both were gulping for air

and trying to focus on each other through passion-bleared eyes. "I've wanted to do that every time I was with you these past weeks. God, it's been hell to keep my hands off you." As he talked, he was nibbling at the tips of her fingers in turn, laving the pads of them with an ardent tongue.

"Why didn't you?"

"To give you space. You weren't ready before."

"Do you think I'm ready now?" Her voice spiraled into nothingness when his tongue seductively delved between two of her fingers at their base.

"If not, have pity, Blair. I'm dying for you."

He kissed her again and the hand that trailed down her side brought a shiver of anticipation over her entire body.

"Cold?" he asked.

"A little."

"Sit up." He pulled her up until she sat between his raised knees, cradled against his bare chest. He draped his discarded T-shirt over her shoulders and slid his hands beneath her arms to meet over her stomach. "You still feel so tiny," he whispered. Erotically symbolic, his tongue probed the small cavern of her ear. "Will you break if I love you?"

"We won't know, will we, until you do?" She took his hand beneath her own and brought it up to cover her breast. "Touch me, Sean."

Where her courage came from she never knew. Where her carefully maintained caution fled to she never knew. Nor did she know when her wall of defense first began to crumble. Her past meant nothing.

The time with Cole could very well not have happened for all the effect it had on this moment with Sean. At this point in time, she didn't want to be reminded of who she was, or who he was, or the opposing directions of their lives. It was suddenly essential that he touch her, that the longing that had plagued her since she first saw him be gratified at last.

His other hand came up to join the first and after closing over her breasts in gentle acceptance of her gift, he fanned them with light strokes. "You're precious. Precious." His thumbs settled on her sides while his fingers cupped the swelling undersides of her breasts. She may as well not have been wearing anything, for the thinness of the leotard masked nothing. He lifted her gently, kissing her neck as he fondled her at leisure.

"I want to see you again," he said as his thumbs came around to circle her nipples with hypnotic repetition. "When I undressed you that night, these were full and erect. Was that because I was there looking at you?" She nodded, then leaned her head against his shoulder, permitting him a better view down her throat.

"I want to watch them grow that way as I touch them. I want to kiss them, taste them, feel them against my tongue, in my mouth, against my face."

She groaned when one hand slipped under the leotard to claim what his evocative words had readied for his possession. The palm of his hand burned against the cool flesh of her breast. The nipple bloomed between his fingers that adored so elegantly.

Moving her chin back farther, she groped for and found his mouth bending toward her, as avid and hot as her own. Tongues skirmished in a passionate battle where all were the victor. And all the while his hand cherished her with a greediness tempered by caring.

As the kiss deepened, he lay back, bringing her with him and turning her over until she was positioned above him. He bartered one pleasure for another. One hand tangled in her hair while the other smoothed up her thigh beneath her skirt. She held her breath when his fingers reached the high leg of her leotard, then sighed with bliss when he didn't let it act as a barrier to his caress. His strong fingers slid beneath the stretched fabric to knead the smooth rounded muscle of her derriere.

Tearing her mouth free of his avaricious lips, she asked, "Sean, why did you take off all your clothes?"

His breathing was sporadic. "To goad you into a reaction. To shock you into some kind of response. To see if I appealed to you at all. Do I?"

She nestled her head on the forest of hair on his chest. His vulnerability was endearing. "Yes, yes," she whispered with her lips against the salty-tasting skin. "You're beautiful. I've always thought that."

"Do you know how much I've wanted you, Blair? Do you know that my body hasn't given me a minute's peace since I first saw you?" He shifted slightly and asked hoarsely, "Do you know how much I want to be inside you right now?" With his hand on her naked buttock, pressing her against him, how could she deny the proof of his desire pulsing against the cradle of her femininity?

She made an adjustment of her own that robbed him of breath. "I think so." Instinct instructed her. She rocked upon him gently.

"Sweet . . ." His head went back and dug a crater into the soft sand beneath the blanket while his eyes squeezed shut and his teeth were bared in what could either be a grimace of intense ecstasy or excruciating pain. "Blair, for godsakes don't do that. I want to make love to you, but not here. Come on."

He rolled her off him and began gathering the remnants of their picnic with quick, jerky movements. She could barely keep up with him as he stalked to the car with his long stride. The wind whipped his hair, the cool evening chilled his bare torso, but he was impervious to the elements as he approached the car with a single-mindedness of purpose.

As soon as the things were stowed in the backseat, he brought the engine of the car to roaring life. Blair sat curled next to him, disdaining the passenger side. Her head lay on his shoulder, her hand on his thigh. The hand alternately squeezed and stroked, growing bolder with each block they traveled.

"You'd better cut that out," he warned when he slammed to a stop at a traffic light.

"Or what?" she dared him on the merest of whispers.

He caught her hand and pressed it to that place that left no doubt as to the unreliability of his control.

"If you want to fondle something, fondle that. It's begging for it."

For a moment she froze, mortified by what he had done. But when the initial shock wore off, she found herself without a convincing reason to remove her hand. Inquisitive fingers threatened his sanity.

"So much for my good ideas," he anguished. "Thank God we're home."

He swung the car into the driveway. The sight that greeted them as he screeched to a stop was totally unexpected and unwanted. Two cars with several passengers each were parked in front of the stairs leading to Blair's apartment. Bodies of each sex were draped in varying poses on the cars. A few were perched on the stairs and bannister. Chatter and laughter punctuated the night air. It looked like a band of gypsies had camped on her doorstep for the night.

And that's exactly what had happened.

Sean's curse seared the roof of the car. "What the hell is this?"

Blair shook off her momentary stunned surprise and scrambled for her own side of the car. "Friends of mine," she said breathlessly, and retreating from his seething eyes, shoved open her door and shouted uproarious greetings that were in direct contrast to her mood.

She was lifted into an adagio hold over one of the young men's heads, then swung from one friend to another to receive a hearty hug. Altogether there must have been twelve to fifteen friends who had driven out to see her, though she never got an accurate head count as they never stood still long enough.

"Where have you been?"

"We've been waiting for hours."

"Is that sand on your toes?"

"Hope we didn't interrupt anything."

Questions and quips were fired at her with the rapidity of machine-gun fire. "Uh," she said, drawing her fingers through her tangled hair, "Sean and I went on a picnic after my classes to celebrate . . . Oh, that is Sean Garrett, my land . . . my friend." She pointed to the tall blond man with the tight, tense expression on his face leaning with deceptive nonchalance against the Mercedes. A dozen or so pairs of eyes were directed at him and greetings were called. He responded with a less than enthusiastic "Hello."

"Well the party you two started on the beach will continue. Lead onward and upward," one of the young men said. He grabbed Blair by the hand, and with one of his hands firmly planted on her bottom, pushed her upstairs. A few weeks ago, she would never have noticed his casual gesture. Now her face flamed with color and she hoped Sean didn't see what the man was doing. At the door she fumbled with her key.

When all had filed in with exclamations of approval of her apartment, she glanced over her shoulder to see that Sean hadn't followed. "Sean, please come on up."

"I wouldn't want to intrude." Why was his voice so chill, when moments ago, he was virtually panting with burning desire?

"You won't be. Please."

"Okay."

Before she could reply or wait for him, she was hauled through the door by someone demanding to know where she kept the drinking glasses. Jugs of wine, already opened and imbibed if the gaiety of the crowd were any indication, were passed around as were slabs of cheese, boxes of crackers, and tins of smoked oysters.

"So what's it like living out here in the boonies?" someone asked over the blare of the stereo which someone else had wasted no time in tuning to an acid rock station.

"It's all right," Blair shouted back, smiling. Where was Sean? Oh, over there glaring derisively at the guy with the punk haircut, tank top, and red bloomer pants. *He's really a terrific dancer*, Blair wanted to inform Sean. "I'm teaching class here."

This produced a howl of disrespectful laughter. "To what? Blimpo housewives and their precious darlings?" The comment brought on another hilarious wave of laughter.

"Well, yes, to housewives and children," Blair said somewhat defensively. "It's really great fun. They all love it. Some—"

"Oh my God!" one of the girls cried, placing her

palms flat against her over-rouged cheeks. "She's turned into a regular schoolmarm." Everyone collapsed in laughter. Blair could feel the smile she had pasted on her face begin to crack.

"No matter what you do, Blair, it can't beat your career in the city, you know," one of the boys said sagely. "It gets in your blood, you know. I'll kill myself when I can't dance anymore, you know."

Blair darted a look at Sean whose shoulder was propped against the windowsill. His smoldering eyes said that he wished the young man who had made that last somber comment would get on with his suicide.

"It shouldn't be much longer," she said, dragging her eyes away from Sean's stony face. "The doctor said—"

"What the hell do they know?"

"Yeah, have they ever danced? Have they ever laid off for six stinking months and then tried to get back in shape?"

"Not to mention a career like Blair's being shot to hell in the meantime," someone else chimed in. "How long a memory do you think those producers have? Six months? Forget it. In six months' time, they'll be saying, 'Blair who?'"

"Now, wait a minute." One of the less loquacious young men stood up and went to embrace Blair. "They're all bloody jealous, Blair. That's all," he said, indicating the others. "You'll be back in a few months' time and dancing better than ever."

Blair reached up and kissed him on the cheek. "Thanks. I hope so."

"I know so."

There was a momentary pause in the chatter, and it was obvious that no one was moved to agree. Blair, swallowing a lump of anxiety, said with forced cheerfulness, "Well, fill me in on all the news."

For the next half hour the subject was less grim as they related current happenings to her and reminisced over shared past experiences. Blair wondered why she no longer felt like one of the insiders. This group that she had been such an integral part of now seemed incredibly young and immature and shallow. They were self-centered to a fault, paranoid, and boring. They talked of one thing only—dance.

Sean was ignored and did his best to remain so. Several times he had to consciously relax his jaw for fear his teeth would crack from the extreme internal pressure he was applying to them. His fists were often clenched at his sides. He wanted to clear the room with one fell swoop; to clear, at the same time, that haunted, terrified, grief-stricken expression off Blair's face.

When at last someone reminded everyone else that they needed to start driving back to the city, the party began to break up. Several hugged Blair, wished her a speedy recovery, and asked her to look them up for lunch or dinner if she came to the city. Others, less sensitive, fled down the stairs, competing for the choicest seats in the cars. They drove out of the driveway trailing blasts of the automobile horns and ribald suggestions that she and Sean could pick up their own party where they left off.

When Blair turned away from the door, she saw that at some undetermined point in time Sean had left, too, leaving her alone. That was fitting. She'd never felt more alone in her life. For a few minutes, she pointlessly roamed the apartment, without conscious thought, without mission, without purpose. Just as her life was.

She had no one. She had nothing. This pseudolife she had been building in Tidelands was just that—a sham. She wasn't a part of life here. Never could be. She had only one thing. Only one thing in her life remained constant.

Suddenly filled with resolve, she yanked up her purse and flew out of the apartment and down the stairs. The car had been returned as Pam had promised Sean. Blair pumped it to life and raced out the driveway and to the studio. She never stopped to think that it might not be wise to go into the deserted building by herself this late at night.

She stumbled to the door and unlocked it. With familiar ease she made her way to the office and plugged in the record player on the small table. She pulled on a pair of tights she kept handy in a drawer and secured the ribbons to a pair of toe shoes around her ankles. Whisking off her skirt, she went to the *barre* and did a preliminary warm-up. Only the light in the office fanned across the vast expanse of empty floor.

Her body was now bathed with a film of perspiration. She selected a record and put it on the turntable. Assuming a position in front of the mirrored wall, she began to move to the haunting strains of the music. At first the tempo was slow and measured, then it gradually increased until Blair was whirling around the room with frenzied abandon.

"What the hell do you think you're doing?" a voice boomed out of the darkness.

Blair didn't stop, nor did her well-practiced movements falter. Without an apology or qualification, she answered Sean's angry question.

"What I was born to do."

Chapter 7

Sean, *alarmed to see her dancing so enthusiastically,* stamped to the record player and lifted the arm, causing an abrupt cessation of the music. The resultant silence was almost as deafening.

Blair, coming out of a series of spins, wound down like the ballerina on a music box, slowly, slowly, until she came to a complete stop. For a few moments she stood, shoulders slumped, head bowed, abjectly despairing. When she raised her head, Sean saw the tears streaming down her face, twin rivers of silver in the arc of light coming from the office.

"Don't stop me," she begged, all vestiges of pride stripped from her. "I must dance. Now. This moment. Please."

"You'll hurt yourself."

She folded her arms over her stomach and gripped hard. "I'm hurting now," she cried.

Sean looked at her with mixed feelings. He thought she had never looked so beautiful. Her hair was cloaking her head and shoulders like a satin veil. The eyes that rained tears were those of a disillusioned child, and he felt a surge of pity for her. She was trying so desperately to disregard an undeniable fact.

At one moment he was filled with rage that she had let a bunch of idiots spoil the happiness she was so carefully constructing; and he wanted to shake her until she realized that their opinion didn't matter. The next moment he was filled with such love and the need to protect her that he trembled like one palsied. His strength meant nothing if he couldn't be strong for her. He felt frightfully weak.

"What do you want me to do?" he asked in a hoarse whisper.

"Put the needle at the beginning of the third selection and help me."

"Help—"

"Dance with me."

At any other time, he would have bellowed with laughter. For if he looked like anything in the world, it was *not* a dancer. A lumberjack, a longshoreman, a roughneck, a football player, a wrestler, but not a dancer. But the pitiable sound of her voice eliminated any thoughts of laughter. He felt only a tremendous sadness that this was one thing he couldn't do for her.

"Blair, I can't. I wouldn't know the first—"

"I'll talk you through it. Really all you have to do is hold and lift me."

He wiped suddenly damp hands along the sides of his shorts. "I could drop you."

"No," she shook her head. "You wouldn't. I know you wouldn't. Please."

The appeal so soulfully spoken couldn't be denied. "All right," he heard himself say. He turned to put the arm of the record player at the end of the second selection to give him time to walk to her.

She was standing in fifth position when he joined her. "Stand behind me. For the first few minutes, the dance is mine. Just turn in my direction. I'll let you know before you have to lift me."

The haunting strains of Rachmaninoff filled the room and she whirled away. She glided around him, her personality changed into the character she was portraying. She embodied a woman in love—sensuous, provocative, dancing for her lover. Each movement was beautifully timed and executed.

"This time when I come close, put your arm around my waist and let me lean all the way to the ground." He held his breath fearing that he'd do something wrong, but was amazed when his huge hand caught her at her waist and he leaned with her until, her legs straight, her head almost touched the floor. Instinctively he seemed to know when to help her rise. She danced away from him again.

"When I come back, put your hands on my hipbones and lift me over your head," she instructed as she spun away from him. He was almost taken off guard when she came running toward him and all but flew over his head as his hands caught her on the flat plane of her pelvis and lifted her up. "Now walk in a circle slowly," she said, her voice gleeful.

He raised his head to see her back arched, her arms spread wide in the soaring silhouette of a bird. She felt no heavier than one. "Lower me easily," she said, bracing her arms on his shoulders. He was shocked when her knees settled against his chest and she slid sensuously down his body until the pointed toes of her shoes touched the floor.

She talked him through the rest of the dance. As the music built to its crescendo, she whirled toward him. "Kneel down on one knee," she said on a heaving breath. The music ended with trilling notes as she did a daring back bend over his right shoulder, her toes resting high on his thigh. Finale.

For long moments after the music stopped they maintained that position. Then Blair stirred and miraculously lifted herself off his shoulder. His hand went to her stomach to give her better leverage. She stood, keeping her back to him. From his kneeling position on the floor, he slowly turned her toward him.

Her face was wet with tears, but they were no longer tears of pain, but of joy. "Thank you. It was . . . beautiful."

"You're beautiful." His hands skimmed her body to reassure him that she was real flesh and blood and not some fairy creature sent from heaven to enchant him. With his palms flattened at the base of her spine, he brought her closer and rested his head against her stomach.

It was a welcomed heaviness and she weaved her fingers through the blond hair to hold him closer. He turned his head slightly until she could feel the moistness of his breath as it filtered through her leotard to her skin. Then his lips moved over her, brushing random kisses over her stomach, abdomen, and then lower to her thighs.

"Sean," she cried, though no sound was emitted. She collapsed onto him. He cradled her in his lap, bent her over his thigh, and kissed her with wild hunger. His tongue plundered her mouth that was all too willing a victim. His hands moved through her hair against her head, down her neck, clutching at her shoulders and upper arms. The only thing that prevented him from being a ravenous attacker was that she was in total compliance and just as starved for him. Her arms wrapped around his neck, bringing his head down for the unskilled fervor of her mouth.

When he came up for air, he rasped, "Let's get out of here."

Within minutes they were wheeling away from the studio in his car, the Delgados' borrowed station wagon abandoned for the second time. There was no possibility of their going into Blair's apartment. The "party" that had occurred there was still too recent, and Sean didn't want her wounds to reopen.

He carried her into his house, through the screened room she so enjoyed and through the lower floor rooms to the sweeping broad staircase. Her head lay nestled against his chest in absolute trust. When he set her down in the large bedroom, she looked up at him shyly. "I need a shower."

He grinned sweetly. "So do I. Through there." He indicated a door across the room and she walked toward it, still wearing the toe shoes that looked awkward on one's feet when not dancing *pointe*. Sean was right behind her and didn't turn on the bright overhead lights, but only a heat lamp that suffused the room with a warm orange glow.

He opened the shower's glass door and turned on the taps. As the room filled with steam, they undressed slowly, their eyes never leaving the other. His shorts and shirt were easily discarded, as were his shoes. He had the privilege of watching Blair as she peeled the leotard and tights down her slender hips and beautiful legs. She tossed them negligently atop the toe shoes.

Boldly, her earlier shyness gone, she surveyed the splendor of his body. He indulged her, not moving as her eyes traveled the length of him, then came back to study his flagrant masculinity. Maidenly fingers braved the space that separated them. Hovering for a ponderous moment, she at last touched him.

Had she been looking at his face rather than at what she caressed so timidly, she might have been frightened by the sparks of light that flared in his eyes and beamed into infinity like lasers. The iron-hard set of his jaw tensed in reaction, and the hands that knotted into tight, white-knuckled fists might have intimidated her. Instead she felt only the immediate stirrings of arousal and yanked her hand back quickly. Her eyes flew to his.

"I won't hurt you, Blair," he promised with fierce sincerity.

She smiled tremulously. "I know." Bending forward, he caressed her lips with his.

He stepped into the shower and pulled her in after him. He let them both get thoroughly wet under the fine spray before he lathered his hands and began to rub them briskly over her back. He smoothed over her derriere, loving the silky feel of her skin against his work-roughened palms. She moaned with pleasure as he ran his hands down the backs of her thighs and knees.

He turned her around and handed her the soap. She returned the favor of scrubbing his back, standing on tiptoe to wash the tops of his broad shoulders. She watched the water trickle past the indentation of his waist, past the curve at the small of his back, over the firm muscles of his buttocks. She couldn't quite garner the courage to touch him again.

When they faced each other once more, he washed her breasts, squeezing them gently between soapy fingers. He dripped bubbles onto her nipples and laughed in delight as they cascaded over the pink tips. His hands moved down over her ribs, her stomach, her abdomen to the delta that deemed her woman. Most of the dark down had been carefully clipped.

He cocked a questioning eyebrow and she answered bashfully, "Costumes." He nodded in understanding. She closed her eyes, grateful for his easily satisfied curiosity. But her eyes sprang open when she felt his hand cup her. His eyes were startlingly blue even in the strange light.

"Put your arms around my neck, Blair," he said. She did as she was told, and buried her face in the matted hair on his chest. His hand caressed her. She groaned as sensation after sensation rippled through her in time to the alluring movements of his fingers. She sipped at the warm water streaming down his chest.

Then he removed his hand and pressed her to him from chest to knees, positioning himself between her thighs.

"Sean," she breathed, reflexively arching against him when she knew the power of his desire. "Sean."

He broke the embrace and cut off the water. He helped her out of the shower within heartbeats of her speaking his name with such pleading and wrapped her in a fluffy, absorbent towel, then blotted her dry. Haphazardly he dried himself.

Scooping her in his arms, he carried her into the moonlit room and, holding her in one arm, flung the covers of the bed back with the other. He settled her on the cool, soft sheets before following with his own body. He turned on his side to face her. "I'm still afraid of crushing you," he said as he gathered her to him.

His lips fused with hers, melding their mouths together and sealing them with heat. His tongue teased along the inside of her lips. "Do that to me," he said urgently. She did and was rewarded with an animal growl deep in his throat. Praise makes one brave. When next their mouths came together, it was her tongue that darted into his mouth, a fleeting, flirtatious thing that drove him mad. "Blair, Blair, God, you're wonderful."

His lips found her ear and blessed it with ardent attention. Strong white teeth worried her earlobe. When his tongue had soothed it, his mustache dried it.

"Please, Sean," she said, turning her head toward his mouth. He knew what her request was before she asked it. He licked at her lips with slow, leisurely strokes. His mustache was a caress of itself as it oscillated over her shiny mouth, taking up what he had deposited. "That feels so good, so good."

She pressed her breasts against the crinkly carpet on his chest. It tickled and teased her nipples until they ached for a firmer touch. She plumped her breast in her own hand and pushed it against his chest, finding the counterpart of his nipple and rubbing it with her own.

A sharp cry escaped his surprised lips and he crushed her to him. His mouth went on an uncharted trail down her chest to her breasts. His tongue beat against her nipples like the wings of a butterfly. Then one was enveloped in his mouth and suckled. She felt that he was drawing her very soul into himself and she let it go gladly.

The pulsing action of his mouth echoed the throbbing in the lower part of her body. As though on cue, his hand slipped between her thighs. Fingers gentle and knowing caressed, stroked, sought, and found with such accuracy, that Blair heard her own labored breathing as that of one suffocating.

Her hand idled down his side to find his naked hip. Unconsciously, her fingers gripped him and pulled him ever closer to that part of her that beseeched not to be left wanting. "Love me, Sean."

"I am," he whispered as he explored the realm that held all the secrets of her body. "I'm loving all of you. Feel me loving you."

The blissful torture went on and on until she was held in a fine sensual net from which there was no escape. Her body surrendered complete control to him. When she clung to him with silent sobbing, when her body undulated with the need to be fulfilled, he rolled her to her back.

Shifting his weight quickly, he knelt to kiss what he had loved and she called his name plaintively, clasping his hair in frantic hands and pulling him up to cover her.

He cautioned himself to be gentle, as he knew she'd not been with anyone since coming into his life. He introduced himself into her body with a tentative probing. When she had accepted that much of him, he pressed deeper. He was watching her face, so he saw her teeth clamp down over her bottom lip at the same time he realized that he had encountered a membrane of resistance.

"Blair." Her name was an astonished, horrified exclamation. "This isn't possible."

Her eyes opened. "Don't stop."

"But—"

"Please, Sean, if you love me at all."

He searched her face, still incredulous, but eternally tender with emotion. "God, yes, I love you. Didn't you know that's what this was about?"

"Then please." Her hands persuaded him with pressure at the back of his thighs.

The hardest thing he had ever had to do in his life was curb his own raging passions, but he loved her too well to frighten or hurt her. With meticulous care, and unheralded sensitivity, he slowly, painstakingly sank into the chaste vault. Her years of body conditioning made it easier than he had feared, yet he remained still until he felt her muscles relax and her tension ebb.

Lifting his head from where it lay beside hers on the pillow, he kissed her mouth softly. Her eyes fluttered open. "Am I hurting you?"

She shook her head. "No." She mouthed the word rather than spoke it. The heady thought of what was happening between them, the wonder and awe of it, left her too weak to speak.

"You're sure?" She nodded. "Why didn't you tell me, Blair?"

"Do you really want to talk about it now?" she asked unevenly.

She felt his stomach shake with silent laughter. "I'd rather bring this to a mutually satisfying conclusion." He ducked his head to plant a solid kiss at the base of her throat. His tongue delved into the delicate triangle there.

Her back arched off the bed. "Do you think you can?" she sighed as his lips plucked at her nipples.

"*We* can. Together."

"I didn't think that could happen the first time," Blair said, her lips barely moving over the warm skin of his shoulder.

"It's rare I'm sure." His index finger was detailing the fragility of her collarbone. "And only then if the man is lucky enough to initiate a sexpot like you."

She gave him a resounding slap on the bottom. He nipped at her ear with playful teeth and tickled the sensitive skin behind it with his mustache.

"Ah, Sean Garrett, you've turned me into a depraved human being in one evening. Kiss me," she implored, catching his head between her small hands and pulling him down to her mouth.

She was still nibbling at his lips when he pulled back and asked huskily, "Blair, who was Cole?"

Her head thumped back onto the pillow and she stared up at him wide-eyed. After they had regained their strength, Sean walked to the bathroom to bring her a damp cloth to make herself more comfortable. He had switched on the bedside lamp and now it shed a soft light onto their flushed bodies. At his question, her face paled significantly. He could see perfect reproductions of the lamp in each of her wide green eyes.

"I told you he was a man I lived with for awhile."

"Forgive me for pointing out that you didn't live together in the usual context of the word."

Her eyes closed against a painful memory. "No. We didn't."

Suddenly remorseful that he had taken that shining animation his lovemaking had produced from her face, he said, "Don't tell me if it's painful."

"No," she said, taking his hand in a firm grip. "I want you to know."

He gave her time to collect her thoughts. His fingers lightly massaged her forehead as he looked down into her beautiful face.

"Cole arrived in New York after I had been there for a few years. I was older than he was. He was fresh out of sophomore year in college. His coming to New York was really a rebellious move against his father who was an athletic coach at his hometown high school. Coach Slater couldn't imagine anything worse than having a son who was a ballet dancer, even though Cole was as athletic and certainly more dexterous than most of the football players on his father's team."

She sighed, took Sean's large hand and laid it on her stomach, absently smoothing the blond hairs that sprung from his knuckles. "Cole had had all the pressure he could take at home, so he came to New York and virtually starved until he found a waiter's job to support his dance classes. I liked him, felt sorry for him, and asked him to share my apartment until he could get established.

"We became increasingly fond of each other. Affectionate. Everyone began to consider us 'a couple.' He thrilled to calling home and telling his father that he was living with a woman, especially an older woman. You see, the one thing Cole wanted to prove to his father was that, despite the fact that he was a dancer, he was also a man."

"And?" he encouraged when she became quiet.

"And in the year and a half we lived together, he was never able to prove it."

She seemed to be shrinking away from him and Sean drew her close and held her tight as though to keep her from diminishing into nothingness. Now he knew why she had been so unschooled in amorous embraces. He had found her naiveté charming and unique, but puzzling in one her age. He had thought it was an affectation, now he knew it was genuine. "What happened?" he asked, resting his lips against her forehead.

"One day Cole decided that he couldn't live with that kind of conflict in his life and threw himself in front of a subway train."

"Dammit," Sean sighed and squeezed his eyes closed with the same pressure that he held her to him. He knew the shattering pain that would have caused her, and were he able, he would have transferred it to himself. "You loved him?" he asked intuitively after a long silence.

"Yes, though I know now it wasn't a romantic kind of love. I think I pitied him and regretted the misunderstanding between him and his parents. To some degree I suffered that same kind of misunderstanding all my life and could relate to it. He needed me to elevate his self-image. And I needed him to tell me how good I was. Not a very sound basis for any relationship. I never took the chance of loving anyone else again. Dancing was the only love in my life."

Sean's heart did a flip-flop. "Was?"

She looked up at him and caressed his mustache with her fingertip. "Don't rush me into making any commitment yet. Only know that until an hour ago, I thought the ultimate feeling came from dancing as perfectly as I was capable. Now I know there are other levels of emotion that I never knew existed."

"I'm glad I was able to turn you on to them," he said with a solemnity that was belied by the glint in his eyes.

She tilted her head to one side and eyed him suspiciously. "You've never told me how you became so adept in the art of lovemaking. Besides the years of practice, was there someone in your past who tutored you?"

His smile remained, but his eyes clouded momentarily. "At one time I thought there might be a Mrs. Sean Garrett, but things didn't work out."

"Oh." That piece of news crushed her and she wished she hadn't brought up the subject. Maybe she was better off not knowing. She might never measure up to that unknown identity.

He smoothed the wrinkle out of her forehead. "Blair, don't read anything tragic into that statement. It was my decision. I don't carry a torch. I rarely think of her, and then with supreme indifference. And someday I may tell you the whole boring story, but not now. Not while you're lying beside me naked and gorgeous."

"You're gorgeous, too," she said, admiring again the solid length of his body from his shoulders to his well-shaped feet. "And not a half-bad dancer." Mischievously, she pinched at the hair on his chest.

He groaned and covered his face with both his hands. "I'd have died had anyone ventured in there and seen me. I'm sure I looked like a clumsy oaf playing with Tinkerbell."

"You did not," she said indignantly, sitting up. "You move gracefully all the time. And . . ." She averted her eyes.

"What, Blair?" he asked, pulling her down beside him again.

"You were there when I needed you. Thank you." Her eyes were shining again with unshed tears.

He dabbed at her moist eyes. "Don't thank me," he said in an urgent whisper. "You are just what I needed, too."

When she awoke the next morning in the wide bed, she was alone. Sitting up and stretching luxuriously, she took stock of the bedroom that she hadn't even noticed the night before. She liked what she saw. Andrew Delgado had told her Sean's bed was big, and it was a full king size covered with a quilted spread. The room was decorated in russet and navy that contrasted beautifully with the eggshell-colored walls in the rest of the house. Wide slatted shutters covered the windows and allowed only a hint of bright sunlight in through the closed louvers. The room was masculine, but far from austere.

The parquet floor was cool on her feet as she tiptoed from the bed to open the door. Listening for any sounds, she crept down the hall and peered over the gallery. She jumped back in surprise when she heard the back door slamming shut. She was poised on the landing when Sean came through the kitchen door into the living room and saw her.

Both were surprised. She because he looked so wonderful wearing nothing but a faded, ragged pair of jeans that snapped a good two inches below his hair-whorled navel. He because never before had he come into his house to see a beautiful naked woman at the top of the stairs, her hair in seductive disarray, her mouth swollen with a well-kissed pout, her breasts pink and warm and full from sleep. The sun shining through the stained glass window made her naked skin into a living rainbow.

She took two steps down, but the intensity of his eyes burning into hers halted any other movement. With a predatory gait, he started for the stairs, dropping the articles of clothing he carried onto the floor.

He took the stairs one by one never touching the bannister, never looking down to check his steps. He was like a sleepwalker, protected from mishap by her entrancing form that drew him like a magnet.

When he was several steps below her, he stopped. His chest rose and fell as he breathed lightly. His eyes dropped from their absorption with hers to look at her mouth. It looked slightly abraded and he silently chided himself for the ardency of his kisses. His gaze took in the gentle slope of her shoulders—the ingrained posture that was an essential aspect of her art, and the softly swelling breasts with their delicate rosy crowns.

On eye level with them, he adored them with his eyes, loving them so intensely, they reacted and grew firm. The slightest trace of a smile lifted the corner of his mustache before he extended his hand to lovingly fondle first one then the other. He leaned forward to nuzzle her with his nose and mustache before kissing her breasts in turn. He filled his hand with one and brought his mouth over the nipple to love. His tongue circled and stroked and rubbed it until he felt her swaying unsteadily and encircled her with his arms.

Still standing a stair beneath hers, his hands caressed her hips while his mouth kissed an erotic map over her stomach. She knew the sweet touch of his tongue that was warm and wet against her cool skin. He took another step down. His hands slid to the back of her thighs and his fingers flexed around them.

More rapid now, his mouth rained kisses down the tops of her thighs, to her knees, down her shins. He knelt and kissed her feet, the callused toes. Working his way back up, she gripped his hair hard as he kissed the inside of her thighs. Then his mouth went on a quest too intimate to be imagined, but that converted her entire body into a pliable container of warm flowing honey.

When she felt herself weakened to the point of collapse, she stumbled up the two steps to the landing and sat down. Sean took the steps necessary to catch up with her. Their ragged breathing reverberated through the stillness of the house.

Standing before her, he waited. Her eyes scaled his tremendous height and met his blazing eyes. They scorched her lips and she wet them with her tongue. The involuntary action caused his heart to visibly pound in his chest. That was his only motion. He remained still. Hoping. Waiting.

Her trembling fingers fumbled with the snap of his jeans and worked the zipper down. Slipping her hands inside, she smoothed them over his taut hips, pulling the jeans lower. His hands came up to caress her earlobes and stroke her cheeks. She leaned forward and kissed his navel, debauching it with a limber tongue. Her fingertips fanned over the tawny nest that joined his thighs and gloried in the life that was rooted there. She kissed him. He trembled.

Gradually they reclined, heedless of the hard floor beneath them. Without unnecessary preliminaries, his body and hers became one. So profound was their need that the storm raged and was spent within a few fleeting, frenzied moments. When breathing had been restored to an automatic response rather than an exerting exercise, Sean lifted his head, smiled tenderly, and said lovingly, "Good morning."

Chapter 8

If Blair could have relived any days out of her life, she would have chosen the day she opened on Broadway with Lauren Bacall in *Woman of the Year* and the Saturday and Sunday she shared with Sean after their first night together.

After the episode on the stair landing that had left them both dazed, she dressed in the shorts and top Sean had brought from her apartment. "I also cleaned up the mess in there. You've got sloppy friends."

Persuading him not to put on any more than he had on, she dragged him into the kitchen where fifteen minutes later they had produced a six egg omelet. Sean carried the tray bearing the omelet, toast, coffee, and orange juice onto the screened porch and they attacked the food, only now realizing how hungry they were.

Contentedly curled up in a corner of the settee, sipping a cup of creamed coffee, Blair eyed Sean suspiciously when he said casually, "Of course, you're going to have to earn my hospitality. I'm going to make you work for this deluxe breakfast."

"By doing what?" she asked warily.

He laughed at her scowling brows. "Nothing illegal. As a matter of fact you might enjoy it."

Her eyes lit up with green fire. "Oh, if it's *that* kind of work—"

"Whoa! I think I've created a monster," he said to the ceiling. "No, you're going to help me paint a room in one of my houses."

She wrinkled her nose. "Slave labor I assume."

"Absolutely, but you get bedroom privileges."

"Painting, huh? I wondered why you selected my tackiest pair of cut-offs and T-shirt to dress me in today. Don't I get a bra?"

"Nope. But no complaining. I let you wear panties."

"The sheerest, skimpiest pair you could find."

"I never aspired to sainthood," he said, his eyes full of devilry.

They cleaned the kitchen with dispatch and while Sean loaded the truck with the tools of his trade, Blair democratically made the bed. She hadn't gotten over her initial aversion to the truck.

"Don't you ever clean this thing out?" she asked,

slamming the protesting door and nearly wrenching her arm from its socket.

"That would take away its character," Sean replied, unperturbed.

The house he was currently remodeling was beautiful, a graceful, century-old construction on an estate with beach frontage. The structural work had been done, but Sean was completing the clean-up work before his clients took over with their decorator.

"I told them I'd paint this room for them because of the high ceilings. It's already had two coats. Today I'm just touching it up."

He hauled in buckets of paint, a roller on a long pole, and trim brushes for Blair to use. They set about their work after Sean had taken her on a tour of the house. The hours passed swiftly.

Near lunchtime, Sean came to stand behind her where she was perched on a footstool. She was working with a screwdriver to reattach the brass plate around a light switch. Concentration on her task had kept her from realizing he had come up to her until she felt his hands molding over her bottom in an audacious caress.

"You've got the cutest little tush," he said, pinching it lightly through the soft fabric of her old shorts. "Anyone ever tell you that?"

"Lots of people."

"Oh? Who? I'll kill them," he growled, sliding his hands under the T-shirt and covering her breasts.

"I'm not going to get this thing back on straight if you don't cut that out," she warned.

"To hell with that thing. Turn around and kiss me, woman."

Trying to look put out, but not succeeding very well, she turned into his arms. She was on eye level with him. "This is nice," he murmured against her cheek. "For once I can kiss you without breaking my back."

"Well if it's that much trouble, we'll just have to stop kissing."

He pulled back and smiled with what she knew to be a dangerous smile. "You'd be amazed at how inventive I can be." His hands went around her to cup her bottom and lift her off the stool. "Wrap your legs around my waist. Now, see how well that works. Of course if you wanted to you could put your arms around my neck." When she complied he said, "What a fast learner you are."

"You big phony! This wasn't your idea. We were in this position the day I escaped the mouse."

"Well, I adapted it to fit the need. Be quiet and kiss me."

They teased each other with quick, nibbling kisses until their desire was rekindled to the point where that wasn't enough. His mouth closed over hers and agilely explored it with his tongue. Dipping into her mouth repeatedly, it evoked other lovemaking and stirred their memories to the hours of the night when they had loved each other.

He could easily support her with one arm folded under her hips. The other hand slipped around to caress her breast. He massaged it with ever-closing circles until his fingers treated the peaked nipple to his gentle loving. "Let's get naked and do this some more."

"Mmmm." She covered his face with tiny kisses that were like droplets of water striking a hot skillet. Her thighs closed around him tighter, her ankles locked behind his back. She felt his passion growing, throbbing, and moved against it.

"Blair, please," he groaned and buried his face in her neck. For long moments they stood thus, clinging to each other tightly, letting their longing decrease to a level they could handle until a more convenient time and place.

Lifting his head from the fragrant hollow of her neck, he asked kindly, "Are you all right?" Looking up at him with languid eyes, she shook her head. He laughed softly. "Neither am I, but we'll have to tough it out for now. One last kiss?"

He kissed her tenderly, barely breaching her lips to stroke the tip of her tongue with his.

"Mr. . . . uh, Garrett. We're here."

Blair's head snapped up to see two workers standing in the doorway, hats in hand, sappy grins on their faces, staring at Sean and her with acute interest. She scrambled to disengage herself and regain her footing. She needn't have made the effort. Sean wouldn't let her go.

"Hello, Larry, Gil. I'd like you to meet Miss Simpson. Blair, Larry and Gil Morris, brothers and two of my best clean-up men."

Did he truly expect her to respond normally to

this bizarre introduction as though they were at a cocktail party and not standing in a very compromising position? "How . . ." She cleared her throat and tried again. "How do you do?" She glared into Sean's smug face.

"Hello. Hi," the two men greeted her simultaneously.

"Blair and I have finished off this room, so it's all yours. We were going out for a bite of lunch. Can we bring you back anything?"

Blair squirmed against him, trying to get down. He held her fast.

"Uh, no. No, sir. We just ate before we came," one of them answered. Larry, she thought.

"We'll be back in a while then to help you. Bye."

"See ya, Mr. Garrett. Miss Simpson."

Sean carried her as they were past the gaping men and out to the truck. "I'm going to murder you," she said through stiff lips.

"No you're not," he said with breezy confidence. "You're going to kiss me again as soon as we get to the truck and between bites all through lunch and then some more."

He was right. That's exactly what she did.

"This is totally decadent," Blair said, scooping another handful of sea water over Sean's leg.

"Yeah, but a terrific way to wash off paint."

"But I don't have any paint where you're washing."

"See? It works."

Laughing, she leaned forward to kiss him.

By nightfall everyone in town knew that Sean Garrett had taken a woman to one of his houses to "help," something that had never happened before. Indeed, it had always been a bone of contention to avid matchmakers that Sean never mixed business with pleasure.

They had helped the Morris brothers, who were responsible for informing a gossip-hungry townsfolk, with the clean-up after returning from a sandwich lunch. Sean had invented jobs to keep them busy until the brothers finally left at sundown. Then he had rushed her to the private beach. His nude cavorting in the surf was no longer a one-man show.

Now they were sitting in the shallow water, the gentle waves washing over them. Blair sat facing him, her legs draped over his.

He bent his head to taste the flesh of her breast. He took a gentle bite, then raised his head and mimed energetic chewing. "Needs more salt," he said, ladling a handful of water over her breasts just to see the nipples contract.

"You idiot," Blair said, shoving his shoulder.

"I love you, Blair."

The words were spoken with such seriousness and the hands gripping her upper arms were so strong that she didn't doubt he meant what he said. She stared at him a moment, his sudden announcement taking her by surprise, then she dropped her eyes to a point on the middle of his chest.

"You . . . said that last night." Her voice was so low that the ocean breeze nearly ripped the words away before he could hear them.

He lifted her chin with his index finger. "Yes, I did. But I was in the throes of passion. I wanted to tell you now, when we weren't making love, so you'd know that I meant it. I didn't plan on falling in love at the ripe old age of thirty-eight, but I'm head over heels and eaten up with it. I do love you, Blair."

"Sean—"

He placed his finger over her lips to silence her. "You don't have to say anything. I just wanted you to know."

The moon rising over the horizon cast a shimmering beam on the water that pointed to them like a spotlight. Its glowing light shone on Sean's blond hair, touching his eyebrows with gold, and making his eyes sparkle. She outlined his face with her fingertips, touching the bushy brows, tracing the length of his nose, following the strength of his jaw to the vertical cleft of his chin.

"It's not easy for you to believe that I love you, is it?"

"Why do you ask that?" High emotion twisted her throat into a tight knot.

"Will you indulge me in a little amateur analysis?" She nodded. "You didn't fit the mold when you were growing up. Because you weren't accepted by your peers, you separated yourself from them, making yourself even more unapproachable than you already were. Your parents didn't understand your artistic obsession with dance. They wanted you to be 'normal.' You've never gotten over the rejection you felt in your youth. Even now that you're a success, you're still constantly seeking approval, acceptance. That's why your friends upset you so much the other night. Their opinions count."

Tears clouded her eyes. How could he see through her so well? How could he speak aloud the things she'd never been able to admit to herself? How had he known exactly how she felt about herself, her life?

Before she weighed the risks, she heard herself speaking. "I was never one of 'the crowd.' I *was* different. My parents, instead of giving me free rein to pursue my interests, saw my interest in dance and theater as a perversity. Why couldn't I be more like my brothers and sisters? I left for New York with an I'll-show-them attitude."

She tossed her head back defiantly and her harsh laugh was without humor. "I still don't meet with their approval."

"I'm sorry," he said. "I know that hurts you. Parental opinions matter, but no one else's should, Blair. Don't you see that you're seeking approval for accomplishments when what you really want is acceptance for being the person you are?"

He lifted her face between his palms. "You're a worthy human being whether you ever dance again or not. Your talent is a gift, and if God saw fit to bless you with it, why should it matter to you what other people think about it? About you? I love you, Blair, but I know you're terrified of that. You've built a wall around yourself that I'm afraid you'll never let me tear down. Will you? Can you? Can you let me love you? Can you love me back?"

Yes. It was possible, just possible, that she might be falling in love with him. The idea of life without him was desolate and dark. He had filled her days with light, laughter, simplicity. Still she was afraid to make a commitment. Love had been too long in coming. The thought of accepting his love terrified her because he might decide somewhere along the line to throw her back and she'd be alone again.

But he had said he loved her. Could she love him? She would ponder that idea, take it out and examine it when he wasn't so close, so overwhelming, so . . . naked.

She placed her fingertip on his lips. Her eyes penetrated the depths of his in a communication of the spirits. She made him the only promise she could. "If I ever let myself love anyone, it will be you."

"What in the world!" Pam exclaimed, having thrown open the front door to greet her guests for Sunday dinner.

"He insists on carrying me whenever possible," Blair explained. "I can't convince him that my legs are practically well."

"We're not sure after Friday night. You might have hurt them," Sean said to Blair, looking directly into her face, wondering why he hadn't missed her before she came into his life. She was such a part of it now, he couldn't imagine having lived all these years not even knowing her. He had loved waking up the last two mornings with her curled against him, barely making a dent in the mattress she was so small.

He couldn't quite believe how soft her skin was, or how shining and silky her hair felt sliding between his fingers. Watching her apply her make-up in his bathroom mirror, he was amazed as she wielded brushes and wands and pencils that highlighted her complexion and eyes. He drove her to distraction with his questions about the contents of each bottle and jar.

He sampled each of her fragrances on a different part of her body, a research project that had eventually concluded on the wide bed with no definite results documented. He decided that her hair, her breath, her skin all exuded a combination of intoxicating essences that no perfume could champion.

As a collection of toiletries and garments began to litter his bathroom and bedroom, he was made aware of how colorless his life had been without these testimonies of a feminine presence. It was a void he hadn't even known was there. But not just anyone could have filled it. Only this tiny creature who had an iron will, but who, he knew, also was frightened and vulnerable at this point in her life. What she had said as the tide surged around them, he had taken as a vow. She *would* love him. He'd see to it.

Looking down at her now, he saw her face soften at his reminder of that momentous Friday night. "But you were there to help me. I couldn't have done it without you."

His mouth settled on her ear and he whispered, "There are a few other things you've done lately that you couldn't have done without me." She giggled.

"Don't mind me, please," Pam said sarcastically. "The two of you go right ahead with your private conversation and little jokes and when you decide to include me, I'll be standing by."

They laughed at her piqued expression as she moved aside to allow Sean to carry Blair inside. Sean's phone had been ringing when he had stepped out of the shower late that morning, leaving Blair to rinse her hair one more time. The call had been from Pam who extended him an invitation for dinner and cards.

"By the way, I haven't been able to reach Blair. Have you seen her?"

He looked in the doorway where Blair was standing. Only a wispy excuse for panties covered her. She was towel drying her hair. "Yeah," he had drawled. "I've seen her."

"Well, tell her she's invited, too."

"I'll do it." A half hour later, the telephone receiver was still off the hook where he had dropped it.

"As usual this house is bedlam," Pam announced to Blair and Sean as she stepped back from the door. "The baby's taking a nap, but Angela and Mandy have been fighting since they got out of Sunday school and I'm sure they'll wake him at any moment. The boys are the proud owners of a new soccer ball and a few minutes ago it crashed into my new lampshade. They've been banished to the backyard for the time being. Sit down."

Sean and Blair laughed again at her harangue which seemed to have been delivered in one breath. Sean made no apologies for taking a seat on one of the Delgados' well-used sofas. He dragged Blair down beside him and tucked her under his protective arm.

A few minutes later Pam carried in a tray with four glasses, a carafe of wine, and a platter of cheese and crackers. "We can nibble on these while the lasagna is baking," she said.

"I can think of a couple of things I'd rather nibble on," Sean murmured in Blair's ear and looked significantly at her breasts.

Joe, who had overheard Sean, choked on his wine. Pam, who hadn't, demanded, "What's so funny? What did he say? What's going on? Somebody please tell me." To her increasing irritation, none of them would satisfy her frustrated curiosity.

Dinner was a rambunctious circus with five noisy, hungry Delgado children as the featured performers. It was still enjoyable due to Pam's good cooking and the loving atmosphere interspersed with laughter and bantering and scolding. After Blair helped Pam with the dishes, they joined the men in the living room for a game of cards.

"Just think, in a few weeks, we can play cards in the playroom," Pam said, waiting as Joe dealt.

"I thought I was building that playroom for the kids."

"Well, they have to sleep sometime," Joe said dryly.

Two of the card players found their attention wandering. Sean's hand had a habit of finding Blair's thigh under the table and roaming at will, until once she dropped her whole hand of cards on the table. Pam stared at them both with open-mouthed confusion as they simultaneously burst out laughing. When the wine bottle was passed around, they toasted each other and then had to be nudged back into consciousness when they found they couldn't break their eye contact over the tops of their glasses.

Finally, when everyone had waited for several minutes for Blair to bid while she stared transfixed at Sean's hand lying relaxed near her own, Pam said in exasperation, "For goodness sake, would you two like to adjourn to our bedroom for awhile?"

Sean and Blair looked up in surprise. Had they been that transparent? Joe chuckled. "Like hell they will. If anyone adjourns to our bedroom, it'll be us. And I'm not into group sex. Besides, you're taking a lot for granted to even suggest such a naughty thing," he said righteously. "I'm sure the idea of a nice, comfy bed never crossed their minds."

Pam grumbled, "I wouldn't bet next month's supply of birth control pills on it."

"Birth contro . . ." Blair's high squeak dwindled to astonished silence as her wide eyes flew to Sean.

He met her own flabbergasted stare with one of his own. Then he shrugged and smiled guiltily.

"My God, I can't believe it," Pam cried, slapping

her hands over her mouth. "The two of you . . . without any . . . Oh!" Uncontrollable laughter stifled the rest of her words until she was able to sputter, "You'd better be careful or you'll wind up with as many children as we have."

"Sean, we can't. Really. I mean it now." Her hands were spread wide on his chest, staving off his ardent kisses.

"I've told you a thousand times," he said, flopping onto his back on the bed and thumping his fists into the mattress. "Whatever damage could be done has been done. One more time before you see a doctor isn't going to hurt."

"And that's baloney. Every high school boy since Adam has used that line."

"Did Adam go to high school? Garden of Eden High?"

Biting back her laughter she said sternly, "Stop changing the subject and don't . . . ah, Sean, please." She took his hand away from her breast and pushed it away. "I agreed to sleep with you if you would behave. I'll leave if you don't stop."

He had the grace to look contrite. Folding his hands behind his head, he said, "All right. I'll keep my hands to myself if you'll take off that nightshirt."

Her look was one of total disbelief. "If you can't refrain from touching me with my clothes on, how do you expect me to believe you'll refrain with them off?"

"You'll take my word as a trusted friend," he said gravely.

"Oh, sure. Just like I'll take your word that one more time wouldn't matter. I know more biology than that, Mr. Garrett."

"Please, Blair," he whined. "I'm naked and since you're not it's making me self-conscious."

She laughed, propping herself up on one elbow to look at him. "You've never known a self-conscious moment in your brazen life." It was a test of her self-discipline not to reach out and touch him. Ever since Pam had inadvertently reminded her that she was running the risk of pregnancy, she had sworn not to let anything happen between them until she could see a gynecologist. She was only getting used to the idea of loving a man. Motherhood was something else again.

"Please. Truly, all I want to do is look."

She sighed wearily in surrender. "All right. But remember, you gave your word." She peeled the nightshirt over her head. "There. Are you happy now?"

"Immensely," he snarled, lunging toward her and pinning her to the bed with his weight.

"Sean, you—"

"Never take the word of a sex-starved man with a naked lady in his bed. That's lesson number one." In between words, he was scouring her breasts with kisses.

"What's . . . lesson number two?" Blair asked, writhing up to offer him better access to her nipples that were distended with awakened sensations. Her earlier resolve was being defeated by the delicious languor that stole through her body under the dictatorship of his hands, his mouth, his knee between her thighs.

"Lesson number two . . . is that . . . there are other ways we can love . . . each other." His mouth and hands worked together to bring her to a pitch of desire more transporting than she had known before. Her own whimpering pleas thrummed through her head as her fingers dug into the muscles of his back. "Are you . . . willing to . . . learn a . . . few?"

The lessons continued all night.

"This isn't going to work," Sean mumbled out of the side of his mouth.

"It's not going to work if you don't sit still." The tiny silver scissors in her hands clipped away an errant whisker. "If you can sit and bug me while I put on my make-up every morning, the least you can do is let me trim your mustache."

He caught her wrist. "But you might trim off more than I'd like."

"I wouldn't cut off one precious whisker that wasn't absolutely necessary." The last word dissolved against his mouth as she leaned down to kiss it softly. He muttered disagreeably when she straightened and raised the scissors again.

When the telephone in the bedroom rang, he sprang from the small vanity stool supporting him, and chortled, "Saved by the bell." He dashed from the room and left her with a satisfied, happy smile on her face.

"Blair, it's for you," he called.

She could read the puzzlement on his face as he extended her the telephone. To her silent query, he shrugged. "Hello."

"Blair, I've been trying to reach you since sunup. Where are you and who was that?"

"*Barney?*" she cried incredulously. The last person she would have thought to hear from was her agent. She had sadly told him not to call her until she had notified him that she had been granted a clean bill of health. He had cursed, paced, ranted and raved, and then treated her to a lunch at which they both got methodically sloshed in order to drown their remorse. "How did you—"

"Pam Delgado. After I traced you through directory assistance for new listings and after I spent hours listening to an unanswered ring, I thought to call her. She said you might be at this number. Who's the guy? Never mind. Are you sitting down?"

As usual Barney's subjects changed direction with the speed of a ricocheting bullet. She had grown accustomed to his hyperactivity and hectic pace since he had become her agent seven years ago, but two months out of the city had slowed down her reflexes and she found herself struggling to keep up with him.

"No, I'm not sitting down, what—"

"How would you like to be in the new show Joel Grey's starring in?"

For a moment her brain didn't register a thing. Then it went into overtime, thoughts racing by so fast she couldn't grasp them. "What . . . that show's already been cast."

"Yeah, but five of the dancers got kicked out over union disputes or something . . . hell, I don't know. What difference does it make? The director called this morning, at an ungodly hour by the way, and asked for you."

"He asked for *me*?" Her hand flew up to still the thudding of her heart.

"Well, sort of," Barney hedged in agent fashion. "He said he needed to see my best girls and you're certainly one."

"Yes, but—"

"You're in the big time again, Blair." He gave her the time of the audition and the address of the rehearsal hall where it was to be. "Get your dancing shoes on—soft shoes they said—and get your butt on the next train to the city. By the way, you may have to sing a song, but you can fake it. Just give them volume."

Sean had pulled on a pair of jeans and a work shirt. Now he was sitting on the edge of the bed they had made up together, staring at her like a conscience incarnate. Caught up now in Barney's excitement, she averted her head. "Do you really think I can do it, Barney?"

"Of course. You're the best."

"I'm not too old for the chorus?"

"I'm too old for dumb questions. Call me when

you get to the city." The phone buzzed dead in her ears. She put it back in its cradle, staring at it a moment while she ticked off the things she had to do before boarding the train. She only had an hour or two—

"What's up?"

She jumped when Sean's voice broke into her whirling thoughts. "An audition," she said excitedly. She paraphrased what Barney had told her.

"You're going?" he asked, a trace of disbelief in his voice.

"Of course I'm going," she said defensively. "This is a tremendous break in my career."

"Um-huh. You might also get a tremendous break in one of your legs."

He was saying exactly what she didn't want to hear. Why couldn't he be glad for her? "I won't. I danced the other night. My legs have never felt better."

"You got lucky."

"They're healed!" she shouted.

"Then you shouldn't mind seeing the doctor before you go to that audition. I'll take you."

"I haven't got time," she said, heading for the door and then rushing down the stairs, ignoring the twinge of pain that caused in her knees. "And I don't need you to take me anywhere. I can find my way around the city."

She heard Sean's curse as he tramped down the stairs after her. "Blair, think for godsakes. I know this could be a big opportunity, but if you get in a show, you'll be doing day-long rehearsals and—"

"I know what doing a show involves and I can't wait to get back to it." He was close on her heels as she crossed the yard and climbed the stairs to the garage apartment. When she went through the door, he followed. She turned to bar his progress any farther. "If you'll excuse me," she said coolly.

Undaunted he continued. "If you won't think of your own health, think of your obligations here."

She laughed. "Oh, come on, Sean. No one will remember me a week after I leave," she said, spreading her hands wide. "Those little dancing classes don't mean anything."

His jaw hardened to stone. "Maybe not to you, Miss Simpson, but 'those little classes' mean a helluva lot to the ladies who attend them. They mean even more to the little girls. You yourself said some of them show real promise. Mandy Delgado for instance. How are you going to tell her you won't be around to coach her anymore?"

His arguments struck her harder than she wanted him to know. "Her talent's inherited from Pam. Anyone could coach Mandy."

"But you'd be the best for her and you damn well know it."

"All I damn well know is that you're keeping me from getting ready for my audition."

"And you'll just leave, drop the classes?"

"Everyone knew they were only going to last for six months at the most," she screamed. "What's the matter? Are you sorry now you made such a heavy investment in the building?''

The lines around his mouth went white and two spots of high color rose to his cheeks. His eyes narrowed as he surveyed her scornfully. She thought he might very well hit her with one of the tight fists clenched at his thighs. Without another word, he spun around and slammed out the door, rattling the window panes.

Three hours later found Blair standing outside the door of the rehearsal hall. Through it she could hear the choreographer calling out the steps of the dance he would teach to those auditioning for the five coveted parts. The piano was as out of tune as any in a dance rehearsal hall, though the song being played was familiar to her.

Despite her angry quarrel with Sean, she had managed to pull herself together and drive Pam's car to the train station in time to catch the next train. Still wearing the scarf that hid her hair curlers, she had taken a taxi to the appointed building at Broadway and West 73rd. She had brushed out her hair in the ladies room downstairs where she changed from her summer skirt and blouse into her leotard and tights.

Not wanting to admit how one encouraging word, one good luck wish, one supportive kiss from Sean would have made this much easier after her involuntary sabbatical, she turned the rusty doorknob and went into the hall.

Chapter 9

"*Blair! My God, what's happened?*" Pam asked in a rush of words. She had answered the tapping knock on the front door to see her best friend standing on the threshold, tears pouring down her cheeks from red, swollen eyes, her eye make-up smudged by previous tears. Her shoulders were hunched forward in a self-protective slump.

"Is Sean here? That's his truck."

"Yes, he's here working on the room, but—"

"I don't want him to see me like this, but I have to talk to you."

"Come on in," Pam said quickly. She hustled Blair through the door and then down the narrow hallways of the house to the back bedroom she shared with Joe. "The baby's in his crib. The others are out playing. Andrew's with Sean. Hopefully no one will bother us for awhile." She closed the door behind them and sank onto the bed beside Blair who was already there, bent almost double and sobbing.

For the time being Pam didn't try to stop the tears. Whatever had happened at that audition, Blair would have to tell in her own good time. When Sean had arrived to work on their room addition, his face dark, his eyes stormy, Pam had bravely asked him if Barney had reached Blair. He snarled an affirmative, then went on in the most blasphemous terms Pam had ever heard come out of his mouth about what he thought of Barney, the audition, and a woman who was too stubbornly obsessed to know what was good for her.

"I take it you don't approve of her going back to the city and even auditioning for a part."

"Damn right!" he roared. "She could end up a cripple."

Well, Blair had walked into the house under her own power, so Pam didn't think her trauma was physical, but whatever it was, it was having a devastating effect. She rubbed Blair's back soothingly, as she would do to one of her children. The words she crooned were sympathetic. The wracking sobs finally began to subside.

"Tell me about it, Blair." Her voice was soft, comforting.

Tear-bloated eyes were raised to Pam's. Trembling lips were stilled by being pressed together hard until they turned white. Then, shuddering in her effort to regain self-control, Blair said in a barely discernible croak, "I didn't make it."

Pam masked her sigh of relief. She felt just as Sean did, that the last thing Blair should do was go back to work before her knees were sufficiently knit. She knew the grueling punishment of dancing every day for hours at a time. If Blair were ever to dance professionally again, she had to give her body time to regenerate.

"Did your knees give out?"

Blair shook her head. "No, Pam, that's just it. I warmed up well, I danced better than I ever have. Ever. I put everything I had into that audition, and . . ." She drew in another shuddering breath to ward off an attack of tears. "My limited singing ability didn't count against me. None of the others could sing well either. The choreographer and the producer narrowed it down from about fifty to eight of us. I *knew* I had made it. I couldn't miss. I had more experience, more credits. I danced flawlessly. I was animated. But I was a good five years older than the oldest of the others. When the choreographer named the five who made it, I wasn't among them."

"Oh, Blair, darling, you know that rejection at an audition doesn't mean anything. It just wasn't your show. You've been x-ed from auditions dozens of times. There'll be others."

Blair laughed ruefully. "I wish I could believe that, but I don't. I *had* to make this one to survive.

Don't ask me how I know that, I just do." She squeezed Pam's hands hard. "I danced so well, Pam. I *did*."

"Much as I sympathize, I hope you didn't hurt yourself," Pam said worriedly. "Do your legs hurt?"

Blair shrugged. "A little. No more than usual."

Pam broached the next subject tentatively. "Sean was worried sick about you. He was pawing the ground like a bull, but he was scared silly you'd fall or that you'd hurt yourself and wind up in the hospital."

Blair scoffed. "He was only angry because I didn't heed his unsolicited advice." Her lips began to tremble again. "When I could have used his encouragement the most, he yelled at me. So much for developing relationships. I guess I'll go down as another notch on his belt. I'm sure I meant no more to him than that anyway."

"Don't say such a stupid thing. It makes me angry, Blair. For once will you open your eyes?" Pam shouted. Blair looked up in amazement. She'd never, in all the years they'd been friends, heard such censure in her friend's voice. "The guy's in love with you. Crazy in love with you. And if you were smart, which I seriously doubt, you'd pay attention to him when he tells you he is. He was out of his mind with worry for you, not if you'd make the damned audition, but if you'd survive it. He and I agree that your health is more important whether you think so or not. He was so upset he called George Silverton just to—"

"George Silverton!" Blair interrupted with an exclamation. *"The producer of the show, George Silverton?"* She came flying off the bed.

Pam was startled by Blair's sudden return to life. She took a step backward and answered cautiously, "Yes."

"And how does Sean Garrett know George Silverton?" Blair demanded.

Pam moistened her lips nervously. Had she opened a can of worms? She didn't like the icy glaze that was forming over Blair's green eyes or the ramrod straightness of her back. "He . . . he, uh, did a house for him last year. They became fairly good buddies, I think, and—"

"Never mind," Blair said, dashing for the door and flinging it open. She barreled down the hall with Pam rapidly stumbling after her.

"Blair, wait. Don't go off half-cocked. He—"

"I know what he did," she shouted over her shoulder. She cursed the tricky latch on the patio door before it gave way. Then like a trooper in some vengeful army, she marched across the patio and stepped through the framework of the new room.

Sean was standing straddle-legged hammering long nails into a two-by-four. He swiveled his head around when he heard her scrambling through the open wall. Several nails were protruding from his lips. Andrew, who was assisting his idol, looked up with a broad grin that dissipated to a frown of apprehension when he saw that his first true love was bristling with fury.

"I want to talk to you," Blair announced in a tightly controlled voice.

Without haste, Sean took the nails out of his mouth. "Not now, I'm busy."

"Now!" she shouted, stamping her foot.

Sean's brows lowered dangerously over the glittering eyes. "I'm busy," he repeated in biting tones. "Besides that I don't think this is the time or place for us to air our differences."

"I don't give a damn what you think or who hears us."

"Well, I do." Before she knew what he was about, he dropped the nails which pinged on the concrete slab, dropped the hammer with a loud crash, and plowed toward her, tossing her over his lowered shoulder.

The air was forced out of her body with a whoosh, but when she regained it, she screamed, "Put me down, you oaf." She wiggled, she kicked, she clawed, she pummeled his back with her fists, all to no avail. He swatted her hard on the rump and it hurt so bad tears sprang to her eyes. She dashed them away before he flung her down onto her back on Pam's bed and slammed the door, sealing them alone in the room.

She catapulted off the bed and faced him with both hands grinding into her hips. "I should have known you'd have the instincts of a caveman, a barbarian. They were bound to surface sooner or later."

"I didn't create a scene, you did," he shouted. "I don't apologize for hauling you around like a sack of flour because you have no more sensitivity than one. Even if you didn't mind Pam hearing what we're about to discuss, you should care that Andrew would. He has a worshipful attitude toward you that I frankly think is misplaced."

"Don't lecture me on my behavior," she spat. "I only want to know one thing." Her chest rose and fell with agitation. She could feel the blood boiling in her veins, surging behind her eyelids and making her see red, thundering behind her eardrums and creating a terrible racket. "Did you or did you not call George Silverton this morning?"

"Yes, I did." His expression didn't change. His inflection was calm.

"Are you a friend of his?"

"Yes. We play tennis when he comes out for a weekend."

His succinct, honest answers perversely infuriated her further. "Did you sabotage my chances of getting cast in that show?"

"No."

"Don't lie to me," she screamed.

"I'm not," he yelled back.

"You are! You called Silverton and asked him, as a 'friend,' not to cast a Miss Blair Simpson. What did you tell him? That he'd be risking my falling down one night during a performance? That I was a handicapped dancer? Or was it something just between you guys? That I was your current bed partner and you weren't quite ready for me to go back to work? What did you tell him?"

The words that tumbled out of Sean's mouth as he raked a hand through his hair would only be found on the walls of the vilest public restrooms. He stood in an arrogant pose, hands on hips, one leg supporting his weight, while he eyed her with mingled amazement and disgust.

"You really think that?" he asked finally, when she was beginning to avoid the blue heat of his eyes. "After the past few days we've spent together, you can honestly think that I'd do something like that?"

His voice had gradually risen to a roar. He threw his head back to look at the ceiling while he drew in a deep, restorative, rage-suppressing breath. His eyes closed when he expelled the air in his lungs on one long, sustained sigh as he lowered his head.

"No, Blair, I hate to disappoint you, but I did nothing of the sort. As a matter of fact, your name was never mentioned. I called George, who, yes, *is* a friend of mine. I knew he was producing that show. I asked him about it. Asked him about the type of show it was, trying to learn just how rigorous it would be for you. That's all. Period. Believe me or not. That's the truth."

"Well I don't believe it," she said to his surprise. "I danced too well. I was great. Something kept me from being selected, and it had nothing to do with my performance at that audition."

"And it had nothing to do with me. Why would I do something like that to you?" His voice contained the genuine bafflement he felt. That she could really suspect him of something so devious was incomprehensible.

She laughed mirthlessly. "With your reputation? Are you serious? If for no other reason, to guarantee yourself a live-in playmate-of-the-month."

Livid color flooded his rugged features and he took a threatening step toward her. "I ought to knock the hell out of you for saying that."

"Well that would certainly be in keeping with your style," she flung back at him.

"Or better yet I ought to throw you down on that bed and make love to you until you come to your senses or at least are rendered speechless."

"Conquer with sex. Is that it? Is that what you've been trying to do these past few days?"

"Not conquer. Persuade. Instruct. Convince. Convince you that there's more to life than dancing on a stage."

"Not for me!"

"Oh yes. For you. You've proved it time and again since last Friday night that you can get a high from making love with me that you never knew from dancing."

"No!"

"Yes! I've seen you shine with fulfillment. I've heard you purr with contentment. Radiate happiness like a furnace. Look at you now. Did dancing make you all that happy today? You've been crying your eyes out. And what the hell happened to your hair?"

Stunned momentarily by the question asked so out of context, she reached up to pat her hair, as though to acquaint herself with what could be wrong with it. "I . . . I frizzed it."

"You mean you did that on purpose?" he asked tactlessly.

Her chin went up defensively. "It looks good from the stage this way. It makes me look younger."

"Younger! Yeah, you look like a young guru."

"I don't need to listen to this," she said, stamping past him on her way to the door.

He caught her arm in a fist like a steel trap and whirled her around to face him. "Yes, you do," he said through bared teeth. "You've needed someone to tell it to you like it is for a long time. You, Blair Simpson, are the most self-centered person I've ever known. Your selfishness is so much a part of you that you don't even see it. It's time you did."

She struggled to release herself. It was futile.

"Do you think you're the only person in the world who's ever had a setback? Did life ever make you a guarantee that things were always going to be rosy? What if you never get to dance again? What then? Is that all there'll be to your life? Will you throw yourself in front of a train like your friend Cole?"

"Let me go," she grated, finally managing to jerk her numb arm free. "I won't give up until I'm a success."

"As what? As a dancer? You are. You've had twelve successful years of a dancing career."

"It's not enough."

"It'll never be enough, because there are other

levels of success and only some of them relate to notoriety and affluence. Others have to do with being a warm, caring, loving human being. And as that, Miss Simpson, you're a miserable failure."

The words were like a slap in the face that actually brought tears back to her eyes. "Shut up!"

"No, you shut up and listen to me. No amount of success is ever going to make you happy because you'll never trust it not to fly out the window. You'll still crave acceptance. And it won't matter a damn who else accepts you, because you'll never be able to accept yourself. That's what's wrong with you, Blair. You don't like yourself."

He was too close to the truth and she threw up every shield she had to protect herself. She had to transfer the pain, the guilt. "How dare you lecture me about something you know nothing about. What do you know of disappointments and setbacks? You sit out here in your cushy little nest and hand down sermons on success. Everything you've ever touched turned to gold. Tell me, King Midas, when you ever knew a day of disappointment and rejection."

"Eight years ago when I went bankrupt and lost everything."

The silence was palpable. Sean's unleashed tension rolled over Blair in waves and choked off her oxygen. He had wished her speechless. He had her speechless now as she stared at him vacantly, trying to absorb what he'd just said.

"Bankrupt?" she wheezed.

"Sit down."

She obeyed him without question, walking to the bed and dropping down. He went to the window, staring out it with his back to her.

"I was thirty years old, building crappy houses and condos right and left. Buying up land for more houses and condos. As you said, I couldn't go wrong. But I did. Everything went wrong—unwise investments, a glutted market, high lending rates, tight money. No one bought the houses or condos. Banks called in their loans. I was down to the socks I stood in. I filed Chapter Eleven.

"Country club friends and investors forgot my telephone number and wished they could forget my name. It makes people nervous to be around someone who's going under for the third time, as though they'll catch the contagious disease he's carrying. Anyway I wasn't much fun to be around anymore. I had to sell the sailboat, the XKE, the Cadillac, the six horses, my tennis racquet and golf clubs." He laughed. "I'm not joking. It got that bad.

"Luckily my father had pulled out a few years earlier. He didn't like what I was doing with the high-class construction business it had taken him a lifetime to build. He was right. Anyway his and Mom's financial futures were secured.

"Through the courts I was able to liquify assets and pay back the debts. Slowly. Very slowly. But most creditors got back ninety cents on the dollar. I moved out here and started over. Worked as a carpenter. Found I liked it, working with my hands, building.

"I scraped up enough money to buy my house

and worked on it on the weekends. Then I bought another and sold it, using my house as an example of what could be done with an old house like that. I think you can piece together the rest. I was very lucky. I got a second chance and managed not to blow it."

He turned to look at her now. "You were curious about the woman I planned to marry. She took a walk when the going got rough, panicked at the thought of being chained to a husband who couldn't keep up his country club dues, not to mention her Bonwit's charge account."

"She just left?" All through his tale, Blair had remained silent. Learning that this man who epitomized self-assurance and success had known such failure and vulnerability had drained her of anger and replaced it with a sort of awe.

"Yes, and at the time I was glad to see her go. That was just one less responsibility I had to cope with. But I was mad as hell that she kept the diamond engagement ring. I was planning on selling it." A trace of humor lit his blue eyes.

"You never saw her again?"

"Oh, yes. Several years later, right after a banker from London jilted her for a richer divorcée, she came out here to see me. She ooohed and aaahed over the houses I had restored. I had just bought the Mercedes, which she trailed greedy little fingers over. The *Times* had just done a feature story about me in the Sunday edition. I was back on the way up. She loved my little houses. She loved my little town. She loved me and couldn't imagine why she'd ever thought she didn't."

Blair didn't hide her repugnance. "What did you say to all that?"

"Nothing. I laughed in her face and sent her on her disgruntled way. I wished her happy hunting. As far as I know she's still stalking for a rich husband with both barrels loaded." He wasn't smiling at his own attempted humor when he came to sit beside her on the bed.

Taking her hand, he laid it in the palm of one of his and marveled over its slender fingers and the faint blue veins threading the back of it. "If one lives to middle age, Blair, he has to go through upheavals. Women lose their husbands and have to enter the job market for the first time; men get laid off from a factory job they've had for thirty years and have to find other work; housewives have to cope with idleness when their children leave home.

"I had to start all over. I didn't plan on ever being happy again, yet I'm happier now than I've ever been. This life I'm leading now was totally unpredicted. It just fell out of the blue into my lap like a gift."

Pam had said something like that to her the day she moved into the garage apartment. About something wonderful for her being planned that she couldn't even guess at.

"I love the work I do. I take great pride in it.

There's a tangible satisfaction in watching something taking shape under my hands. I never knew that kind of satisfaction by acquiring a parcel of land that really meant no more to me than the printed deed." He tilted her chin up to peer down into her face. "Do I sound like a complete fool? Maudlin?"

She shook her head. "You sound like a man with both feet on the ground, who knows values by having learned them the hard way. A survivor. A man pleased with his life."

"In all areas save one. My life lacks something vital," he said softly. He lifted the mass of hair covering her ear and brushed his mustache along the fragile rim.

Involuntarily her head fell back and her eyes closed. "What vital something would that be?" She was dimly aware that he was lowering them into a reclining position. Their legs dangled over the edge of the bed.

His mouth maneuvered its way over her cheek to ghost against her lips as he spoke. "A woman to love me. To live with me and share my life. To make laughter and love with." His tongue flicked at the corners of her mouth before gliding along her bottom lip. "Blair, you've been hurt today. If I could, I would have spared you that, but maybe it's better that this happened."

It was hard to think while his tongue was gently probing past her lips and while his hand was playing with the buttons on her blouse, but his conciliatory tone jiggled a nerve that wouldn't let her relax completely. "Why better?" she asked.

"Because now you know you're better off accepting your life here. Now you can forget about ever going back."

She turned her head, dragging her mouth from beneath his. The hand plucking at the buttons on her blouse was caught by hers and removed as she sat up. She twisted at the waist to look back at him.

"I don't *know* anything of the sort, Sean. And I'm not forgetting about anything, especially my career." He came up on one elbow. "You've been telling me for the last half-hour how wonderful and rare second chances are. I've got to make my own second chance. I've got to go back. As soon as I contact Barney—"

"I don't believe this," Sean bellowed, rolling off the bed and driving one fist into his opposite palm. "I've been talking about a second chance with another life, not the same one. Don't be obtuse, Blair. You're only hearing what you want to hear and twisting it to suit you."

"Look at who's accusing me of twisting things. The story you've just told me applies to your life, Sean, not mine."

"They could be one and the same." The simple clarity with which he spoke panicked her more than his earlier forcefulness had done.

"But they're not. Not now, not until—"

"Not until you're too crippled to dance anymore? Maybe even to walk?" He was shouting now.

He turned his back on her and strode to the door,

nearly tearing it from its hinges as he swung it open. "Well, forget that, doll. Forget hobbling back to me. I won't want you by the time you're too battered and beaten to be valuable to anyone else."

The parting words flung over his retreating shoulder were repeated in her head like a satanic chant and held sleep at bay. She tossed on her sofa bed, so uncomfortable and lonely after the nights she had stayed with Sean. They had slept cradled against each other like pieces of a puzzle in his spacious bed. His breath had warmed her ear. His arms had sheltered her. His hands . . .

Pam, laconic and disapproving, had driven Blair home, saying she might be needing her spare car the next few days. They said terse farewells. She hadn't seen Sean as she left Pam's house. She'd only heard the furious cadence of his hammer as he pounded out his wrath on unfortunate nails.

She didn't want to concede, even to herself, how much she was going to miss him. For she had decided on the trip back to her garage apartment that she was moving back to the city immediately. It would be impossible to live within the shadow of his house, seeing him constantly, with this antipathy crackling between them like a spark, threatening to explode into an inferno that would consume them both.

She had begun packing that afternoon as soon as Pam had returned her to the apartment. Tomorrow morning she'd call Pam and explain why she couldn't continue teaching the dance classes. She belonged in the city where she could be on hand should anything break like today's audition. Barney, when she'd notified him tonight, had been ecstatic.

The second thing she didn't want to admit to was the throbbing pain in both her knees. The emotional tumult of the afternoon had kept her from noticing it at first, but once she was alone, the increasing pain couldn't be denied. She had used heating pads and ice packs alternately to no avail. She had taken three aspirins together, then two hours later had been driven to take three more. Cursing and tears of frustration had done no good either. She had danced full force today, holding nothing back. She'd had to dance the lively routine repeatedly. Now she was paying for it. Sean would probably be pleased to know that she was feeling very battered and beaten.

Sean, Sean, Sean. Why did she crave the touch of his hands that soothed and aroused with equal aptitude? Why did she long for the seductive power of his mouth beneath that luxuriant mustache? Why did her hands long to knead the muscles of his back and shoulders, her fingers to lace through the hair on his chest, her lips to taste his own distinct essence, her body to—

"Damn!" she cursed the tears that welled in her eyes. Why was she crying over him more than she was her injured knees? His rebuke had been much harder to take than the rejection at the audition. Why?

There was only one answer and she wasn't ready to acknowledge it.

The telephone jangled loudly near her ear and jarred her out of sleep. She moaned and buried her face in the pillow. It had taken her so long to fall asleep. How dare someone wake her up early after the night she'd had. The telephone rang again.

She pried her eyes open and saw that it was later than she first thought. Her clock indicated a few minutes past ten.

Her arm was tangled in the covers, and she worked with uncoordinated movements to free it in order to answer the telephone that continued to ring stridently. "Hold your horses," she grumbled as she lifted it off the base and pulled the receiver to her ear.

"Blair!"

The voice she wanted most to hear. The voice that had haunted her all night was now speaking to her, but . . .

"*Blair?*" he shouted impatiently.

"Y . . . yes? Sean? What—"

"Is Pam with you?"

Befuddled, she looked around the room, almost thinking she might find Pam there. "No, why? She—"

"Have you seen her? Do you know where she might be?" he demanded rudely.

"I . . ." She wasn't surprised that he was still angry, but this wasn't like him to call and be deliberately rude. "Sean, is something wrong?"

"I've got to locate Pam or Joe. Andrew's had an accident. He's hurt."

Chapter 10

She stared into space, blinking stupidly. "An accident . . . ? What—"

"I was working on their roof. He climbed a ladder to bring me a sack of nails. The damn thing slipped and he fell. Hit his head on the slab. He's unconscious and bleeding all over the place."

A trembling hand was pressed against her lips. Andrew—bright, vivacious Andrew—unconscious and bleeding? *No, no.* "Has . . . has he moved? D . . . did you call an ambulance?"

"No, he hasn't moved and yes, I've called an ambulance. It's on the way. Pam left with the other children about an hour ago. Joe's sergeant is radioing him.

I thought if I could head Pam off she could meet us at the hospital."

Pam! Blair's heart constricted with the thought of what it would do to Pam if Andrew were seriously injured or . . . She clutched at her chest, imagining her friend's pain. Sean said, "I've got to find her."

The telephone went dead in her hand.

God, please no, she silently cried. *Not Andrew. Not Pam. He'll be all right. He has to be. Sean is there. Sean will—Sean! He's alone, desperate. He adores that boy.*

Shoved into action by some invisible, compelling hand, she lunged out of bed, crying out in pain when the hard contact with the floor shimmied up her shin to slam against her kneecaps. She gasped, trying to dodge the rockets of pain that threatened to make her nauseous.

Groping her way to her bureau, she found a pair of shorts and a T-shirt. She shoved her feet into sandals and, disregarding the pain, dashed out the door and down the outside stairs.

"Oh, damn! The truck." Where she had expected to see Sean's Mercedes, the motorized relic was parked instead. She didn't have time to lament.

Reaching the bottom step, she leaped toward the ancient truck and jerked open the door. Sean had told her he always kept a spare key under the seat and, not even thinking about the filth under there as well, her searching fingers located it within a matter of seconds. She crammed it into the ignition and, praying that she would remember how to drive a standard transmission, turned it. Nothing.

"Damn!" she cursed. "Come on and start, you stupid truck." Her feet were working the clutch and accelerator alternately to no avail.

Blair lay her forehead against the steering wheel and gave in to the tears that had been threatening since she had first heard Sean's voice on the telephone. Flinging her head up, she gripped the steering wheel with both hands and shook it. "I've got to go to him. I've got to. Now, damn you, start!" she screamed. All her heartache, frustration, pain and despair poured into that curse. "Start!"

Giving the truck one last useless chance, Blair thrust the door open. She looked around her frantically, hopelessly, wringing her hands impotently. Her eyes swept Sean's backyard, and like a neon sign had pointed it out, her brain registered the alleyway running down the side of the house. "The shortcut," she whispered. Andrew's shortcut. He'd bragged about it, told her how he'd already worn a path through the backyards and alleys to cover the blocks from Pam's house to Sean's.

Driven by some internal force, Blair started off at a run down the alley. She didn't think about the pain shooting up from her knees into her thighs, through her vital organs, along her spine straight to her brain. Indeed, she didn't even feel it.

Precious little Andrew. He loved her. Pam had said so. Pam, her best friend. Pam, whose sound advice and common sense she had often ridiculed, might be facing a crisis. She had always leaned on Pam's strength. It was time she returned the favor.

Had she ever told Pam how much she valued her friendship? And Sean. He loved her. Or had, until she'd rejected his love. *Don't give up on me yet, Sean. Please.*

Through backyards and alleys, she ran. Blair was oblivious to the curious stares of people working in their gardens or pausing in household chores to peer out the window at the woman running at a dead heat. She couldn't be mistaken for a casual jogger.

She didn't see the weeds that slashed at her bare legs or the stones that would leave bruises on her heels and the balls of her feet. She saw only Sean, coming out of the sea, naked and alive and radiating life, exuding a confidence he could share with her.

She didn't hear her labored breathing crashing in her chest. Sean's laughter boomed in her ears to the rhythm of her footfalls; his whispered words of love were the reason behind her thudding heart. Those words had become a salve to her shattered spirit.

The perspiration that ran in myriad uncharted rivulets down her body went unheeded. Instead she felt Sean's caresses, tender and loving, strong and supportive.

How had she thought she could live without all he had to give? She had to get to him, tell him, show him she could be loving and caring. She *did* love, *did* care. This was one time in his life when he might need her. She couldn't—mustn't—let him down. Run! Only one more street.

Her legs pumped faster, working like the pistons of a well-oiled machine. She could see the skeletal framework of the roof Sean had been working on. *Thank you, God. Thank you, God. I'm almost there*, she prayed as she ran the last few yards.

She burst through the hedge of the house that was across the street from the Delgados'. Then everything went into slow motion. Blair saw them—Sean, Pam, and Joe—huddled over Andrew. He was sitting on the step on the front porch, a bloody cloth covering his forehead. He was all right! Wasn't he? He wouldn't be sitting up . . .

Joe looked up. Seemingly from far away, she heard him shout, "Blair!"

Pam and Sean turned to her with the floating maneuvers of characters in a dream. Astonishment and horror twisted their faces into ugly grimaces. They ran toward her, but gained no ground. She saw her name formed on Sean's lips, but didn't hear any sound.

She didn't know that she was running in a crouched position, her knees bent at a hideous angle, barely supporting her. She felt a dull thud as her body struck the sidewalk when she collapsed upon it. She looked down, surprised to find herself on the hot concrete.

Then, for the first time in her life, she fainted.

"Absolutely not!"

"But Pam—"

"Don't 'but Pam' me. I've told you this house is open to you if you want to recuperate here. I'll carry your bedpans. I'll cook your meals, wash your clothes, give you back rubs, anything. But I will not move you out of that apartment."

"Some friend you turned out to be," Blair complained from her sitting position in the bed.

It was four days since Andrew's accident. Andrew was fine, proudly sporting a large bandage on his temple. Blair had progressed to sitting up with a pillow under her knees. This morning she had refused to take the pain pills the doctor had prescribed. Her knees were barely aching and she had celebrated by asking Pam to dress her in a blouse and a pair of slacks.

Pam had put her in a tiny room that was too small for a bedroom but too large to be classified as a closet. It had served as a sewing/storage room. How Joe had squeezed the twin bed in there, Blair never knew. When she had come out of her faint, smothered by pain, she'd been lying on it. For two days, the wracking pain had made her oblivious to her surroundings. Yesterday, she thought she might survive. Today, she was sure of it.

"I *am* your friend. I'd trust you to spend a weekend with my husband and know that nothing would happen, but I'll not do your dirty work for you. If you want to move out of Sean's apartment, out of his life, then you'll be the one to pay off your lease and hand him the key. Not me."

Pam huffed to a chair, the only other piece of furniture in the room, and plopped down, glaring at her friend with exasperation. "The two of you are driving me nuts, did you know that? He's been avoiding this part of the house like we all had the plague or something. He comes to work on the room addition. He leaves. He growls at anyone who gets in his path. He looks like hell—almost as bad as you do."

"Thanks," Blair cut in on the tirade.

"He thinks you despise him."

"Despise—"

"Oh yes. He's thinking about as rationally as you are these days. Since you ruined your knees running to help him with Andrew, he naturally assumes that you'll never forgive him for calling you that morning."

"That's insane."

"Insane the lady says," Pam addressed the ceiling. "Do you see now the kind of whackos I've been dealing with the past four days? And you don't want him to see you this way because he said—in anger—that he didn't want you hobbling back to him crippled. Well, I've had it," Pam said, jumping to her feet. "As I said, my home, my family, *I* am at your service until you get on your feet, but I just resigned as Cupid or Venus or whatever part I've been playing."

Oozing righteous indignation, she stalked to the door. "By the way, your mother called me to ask if you were glossing over what the doctor told you. She'll call you back in a day or two."

Blair extended her hand with a pleading look in her eyes. "Pam?" The other woman crumpled and she returned to the side of the bed to take Blair's outstretched hand. "Thank you for everything."

"What made you pull such a dumb stunt, Blair? You knew that running over here like that would ruin your legs."

Blair shrugged, sniffed back her tears and met Pam's concerned eyes. "I love you."

Pam had tears in her eyes, too. "I love you, too." The next few passing moments were rife with emotion. Then Pam said with soft intensity, "Let me call Sean to come in here to you."

Blair shook her head. "No. It's better this way."

Pam dropped her head. "That's *your* opinion of what's better." With that, she left, obviously still miffed by what she considered to be sheer stupidity on the part of two who should know better.

"Come in," Blair called when someone tapped on her door later that afternoon. She expected to see one of the children with yet another soulful creation of crayon marks on a sheet of manila paper. Her collection of such artistic renderings, the subjects of which were known only to the artist, now numbered eighteen. She was ready with an exclamation of surprise and praise on her lips. It died a sudden death when Sean stepped through the door.

For long moments four ravenous eyes gorged themselves. Looking for signs of suffering, they surveyed each other thoroughly. The diagnosis of each was that physically they were fine, but lines of strain, and pinched eyesockets testified to an emotional malady that refused to heal.

"Pam said you wanted to see me," he said quietly. He barely fit between the foot of the bed and the door.

"She—" Blair bit back her denial. The turbulence in his eyes was painful to see. He needed so badly to be forgiven, to be absolved from the guilt of bringing on her latest setback. For an instant her eyes dropped to the knotted white fingers in her lap. "Yes, I . . . I . . . she said you blamed yourself for this." Her hand swept down to take in her knees. "Sean, you mustn't."

"But I do," he anguished. "If I hadn't asked Andrew for those nails, he wouldn't have stitches in his head and if I hadn't called you looking for Pam, you wouldn't be in here, feeling untold pain and—"

"I'm not in pain. Not anymore. And if I obey the doctor this time, I won't be again. It wasn't just running to Pam's house that brought me to this lowly state," she said with a soft laugh. "It was a combination of things. All of which you warned me against by the way."

She coaxed the slightest smile from him, but he wasn't ready to redeem himself. "Thank God Andrew only had the breath knocked out of him. I thought he was unconscious because of the blow on the head. By the time Joe got here, he was lucid. When Pam arrived, she scolded us for using one of her best towels to stanch the blood. While she and I . . . while she took care of you, Joe drove him to the emergency room for his three stitches."

Blair laughed. "Pam says that bandage will rot off before he'll take it off."

"I wish it were that simple for you," he said quietly. "What does the doctor say?" He knew. He had accosted him as he left the Delgados' house. Pam had called the doctor as soon as she and Sean had undressed Blair and gotten her into bed. She demanded that he come out to Tidelands as Blair wasn't fit to come into the city. He agreed, but at an exorbitant fee.

When the doctor had politely but firmly told Sean that he valued his practice too much to discuss a patient's condition with an outsider, Sean had been all too ready to tell the doctor just how much of an insider he was and that if the doctor valued his life as much as he did his practice, he'd better start talking. Swallowing around the iron fist that had made a garrote out of his Cardin necktie, the doctor had told him what Blair could expect for the next several months.

"I'm not to stand or walk on my own for two weeks, then I can start with short distances and gradually build up. I have to go to the hospital several times a week for ultrasonic treatments. He also recommended taking cortisone shots, but I don't want to. And I refuse to take pain pills," she said adamantly.

She ignored his snort of disagreement and went on. "In a month or so, he'll reassess the situation." Her voice changed. "If everything's healing well, I can start to build back my strength. If not," she said gruffly, "I may have to have surgery. That would entail months of therapy, and I'd more than likely never be able to dance again. At least not professionally."

He was quiet for a moment. Her prognosis matched the doctor's to the letter. He watched her as she picked at a loose thread on the bedspread. "And if you had this surgery and all that it entailed, would you be devastated?"

"Yes." She was still looking down so she didn't see the agonized expression that tore across his already ravaged face.

"I see."

"Because you said you wouldn't want me anymore if I wasn't any good to anybody else. If I was—"

"Blair," he cried, rounding the bed and falling to his knees beside her. "Is *that* why you'd be inconsolable? Because you'd think I didn't want you anymore?"

She nodded. "I would be a physical wreck, Sean. I'd have to be waited on, I'd have scars, I'd have to use a wheelchair until—"

"Blair, Blair," he said, burrowing his face in her lap. "I don't care if you have to crawl on your belly. I'll always want you."

"But you said—"

He raised his head, his agony apparent. "Forgive me. A million times since then, I've cursed my ability to speak for saying such an insensitive thing to you. I was mad, frustrated, loving you so much it was killing me, and dying because my love wasn't enough for you."

She closed her hands around the golden head,

sinking her fingers in the fleecy hair. "It is, it is," she said with a sense of desperation. "I was such a fool, Sean. Spoiled and selfish. Forgive me for not accepting your love, not knowing how to love you back. It had never happened to me before. I was afraid of commitment to anything but dance. *That* I knew. *That* I could cope with. I found a heaven with you I didn't know existed. If having banged-up knees is the only way I could realize it, then it's really a very small price to pay."

His large, roughened fingers smoothed along her temple. "Darling, I hope you dance again. I want you to. Never think I wanted you to stop for any other reason but because it was injurious to you. When I saw you falling, lying there on the concrete, I thought I'd die, Blair."

"I know you'd like to see me dance again," she said, smiling as she traced the groove that adorned his chin. Then her fingertip delighted in the bristly feel of his mustache. "If nothing else, I could be one of the best coaches on the East Coast. And I've got the dancing school here, don't forget. It may have to be suspended for awhile, but as soon as I'm able—"

He placed a finger over her lips. "Don't get too ambitious. I don't want you to ever be disappointed again."

"I won't be, I promise. As long as I have you."

"You do." He kissed her mouth softly, then her neck, her breasts through her blouse, her stomach. He staked small claims, marked his territory, assuring himself that she was real and whole and loving him.

When she tried to speak, her breath came in short spurts, the magic of his mouth having a dramatic effect on her faculties. "My parents will be . . . disappointed."

"Why is that?" He looked up at her.

She lowered her eyes to study the stitching on his collar. "Well, they're old-fashioned. They didn't know about Cole. I don't think they'd approve of my . . . our . . ."

"Living together? I'm old-fashioned that way, too." The quiet words struck her heart with the impetus of lightning. She met his sincere blue eyes with tear-laden green ones. "I've never lived with a woman, Blair. That particular privilege was reserved for my wife. At least I hope you'll think of it as a privilege. Just as I hope you'll consent to being my wife."

She nodded eagerly. "Yes, yes."

He slid one arm beneath her knees and the other behind her back and lifted her off the bed. Trustingly she linked her arms behind his neck. "Where are we going?" she asked, laying her head on his shoulder.

"Home," he said softly.

They passed Pam in the hall. She was slyly smiling.

"That was wonderful. You're getting better and better," the languid voice hummed.

Strong hands rolled her from her stomach to her back and adjusted the pillows behind her. A quick kiss was dropped on the tip of her nose. "I should be. Two massages a day since we got married. Do you think we've set a record?"

"I feel certain we have." Green eyes shone up at him. "But not with massages." She raised her head for a more satisfactory kiss.

It was their fifth night as husband and wife. She was well established in the house, and wondered how she had ever been happy living anywhere else. He carted her from room to room, up and down the stairs, neither complaining nor listening to her constant apologies for the necessary inconvenience. He didn't consider it such. Lying together in the bed, that for so many years had gone unshared, was just one of the many pleasures life was now affording them.

Finally ending the kiss, he eyed her studiously. "Tomorrow I'm taking you outside in the sunshine. You've got a pallor."

"Somewhere private," she said mischievously, dragging the sheet down from her breasts.

"Why?" he asked, his eyes narrowing suspiciously.

"So I can sunbathe in the raw. You don't want me to have unsightly strap marks, do you?" Her eyelids fluttered flirtatiously.

Leaning down and placing his mouth directly over her ear, he drawled, "If I were to do that, you'd end up with no suntan at all, and I'd have sunburned buns." He laughed at her prim expression, which he knew to be fake, and kissed her soundly.

"Did I hear the telephone ringing earlier?" she

asked breathlessly when he freed her mouth. He had taken the extension out of the bedroom so she could rest for an hour each afternoon. Only when he had to be out did he plug it in beside the bed so it was accessible to her in case of an emergency.

"Barney called."

"And?"

"I told him to go to hell."

She laughed. "I'll get back to him in a day or two. His feelings get hurt easily."

He wasn't really worried about her talking to the agent. She'd convinced him that she wasn't bent on dancing again until she was certain her legs could take it, and only then if every other area of her life was being given its priority. It was still a few days until she could begin walking. They weren't rushing anything.

"Andrew called to say that he, Angela, and Mandy colored pictures of the wedding for you. His is the best because in Angela's you're taller than I am and Mandy spilled Kool-Aid on hers." They laughed. Blair loved the sound vibrating against her ear as he held her close.

"Your parents called to say that they had gotten home safely and to check on you." His hand stroked her stomach leisurely, but with tender possessiveness, not passion. "They're very upset about the possibility of your not dancing again. Your mother told me at the wedding how proud they've always been of you. They are, Blair. They just never verbalized it. They're fallible, just like all of us, and couldn't help missing you and wishing you lived closer to them and resenting what had taken you away."

She blotted her eyes against the furred skin of his chest, dampening it with tears. "She really said they were proud of me?" He nodded. With a conscious effort, she pushed the tears aside. She wanted to look forward, not backward. "It was good to see them. They were happy to see me get married at last. And, of course, were most impressed with you." She kissed him under the chin.

"My parents, who can't quite believe I finally talked someone into marrying me, think you're either mentally deficient or a saint. They loved you on sight and told me how beautiful you are. I thought it was a terrific wedding, considering that Pam and I pulled it together within a week."

"It was a strange wedding having the bride sitting down through the whole ceremony."

"And lying down through the whole honeymoon."

She pushed against his shoulder in mock consternation. "Don't you ever think of anything else?"

"Not since you took up residence."

She propped herself up on an elbow to better see him as she combed through his thick hair with loving fingers. "I must say you exercised magnificent self-discipline by sleeping in the other bedroom the week before the wedding."

"I think the least I deserve is the Medal of Honor," he chuckled, but nestled her against his body before he said softly, "I wanted our marriage to be unsullied. I wanted you to know that I love you for many more reasons than what you do to my libido. And, as has been the case since I first met you, I was afraid of hurting you."

He lowered his head to kiss her sweetly on the lips, but after a few moments it grew into something else. He growled against her mouth. "But now that you're my wife, look out, Mrs. Garrett."

"You've got me at a terrible disadvantage. I can't even run from you."

His laugh was a warm blast of air against her cheek as he enclosed her in his arms. "That's good to know. You were long in convincing that I loved you."

Tiny love bites were taken out of his neck by delicate lips and teasing teeth. "My heart and mind were on something else. It took a while to divert my attention from that. And when I really started listening to you, what you said frightened me. It required so much of me. I wasn't sure I was up to it."

"Now?"

"Now loving you and making you happy is the most exciting challenge I've ever faced in my life."

His lips branded an urgent message into her temple. "I love you, Blair."

"I love you, Sean Garrett." She began to giggle and he raised his head to look down at her.

"That's funny?"

"You must know how much I love you if I'm willing to go through life with a name like Blair Garrett."

"I've always had a poetic nature."

She sobered and watched with interest as his

teeth caught her wandering finger. "Sean, are you sure I'm not taking up too much of your time these weeks that I'm an invalid? I don't want you to neglect your work."

"I'm caught up except for the Delgados' room addition and it's being finished by quality craftsmen. I'm overseeing them. The other clients I'm under contract to were understanding about a man wanting to take a few weeks off for his honeymoon. Besides I don't dare leave you alone for too long. You might decide to call that fresh young masseur from the Y. I'm sure he's just itching to get his hands on someone who looks like you."

"I'd never be as threatened by him as I was by you. You had your nerve that day. What made you do it?"

He grinned. "I had to touch you. First to see if you had any substance at all or were just a figment of my lecherous imagination. You looked like such an airy little thing despite the sparks shooting out of your green eyes. Then pure animal lust took over. I wanted to touch you all over." He trailed his mustache along her collarbone. "I'm not over that seizure of lust yet."

He kissed her deeply, his tongue rubbing against hers with increasing ardor. All the sweetness of loving him flooded through her until she was drowning in it. She escaped the fervor of his mouth and dragged his head down to clasp it possessively against her breasts.

"Sean, Sean," she whispered, "I love you so much it frightens me."

He struggled against her frantic hands so he could look at her. His blue eyes pierced through her. "Why? Why, Blair?"

"Because I might lose you."

His expression softened and he stroked her lips with his thumb. "No. Never. Not if I have anything to do with it."

"Love me," she begged.

He needed no second invitation. His eyes navigated each inch of her. She felt their heat on her skin as he looked at her breasts, dwelled on her nipples. His fingers enjoyed the feel of her. Her flesh generously responded. His eyes slid lower over her stomach and navel. The texture of her skin and the white down that sprinkled it were adored by stroking fingers.

"Lovely," he whispered when his eyes encountered the dusky delta that harbored her womanhood.

"Touch me." Her request was a profession of love, as was his intimate, probing caress.

"Here?"

"Yes, yes, yes. Oh, Sean . . ."

"You're so beautiful, so dainty. Sweet." His tongue painted her nipples with dew before he sipped it up with his lips. His mouth sampled morsels of flesh that melted against it until she was consumed with a fever for him.

"Sean, let me . . ."

He gasped as a shudder of pleasure rippled through his body. He recited a litany of love words as she unselfishly loved him. Then he tensed with supreme restraint and rasped, "Blair, now or—" He was welcomed into the tight fluid warmth of her dear body.

"Ahhh, Sean my love, my love." A fervent mouth sought her breasts, kissed them, loved them. Her fingers gripped the hard muscles of his buttocks, entreating him not to withhold any of himself. "Sean . . . I never . . . a gynecologist . . ."

He levered himself up, his eyes burning with passion, but glowing with love and understanding. "My Lord, Blair. I'd forgotten all about that. Do you want me to—"

"No, no," she said, shaking her head, a brilliant smile breaking over her face. "We've got a good choreographer. Let's wait and see what the next steps will be."

ABOUT THE AUTHOR

SANDRA BROWN began her writing career in 1980. After selling her first book, she wrote a succession of romance novels under several pseudonyms, most of which remain in print. She has become one of the country's most popular novelists, earning the notice of Hollywood and of critics. More than fifty of her books have appeared on the *New York Times* bestseller list. There are seventy million copies of her books in print, and her work has been translated into thirty languages. Prior to writing, she worked in commercial television as an on-air personality for *PM Magazine* and local news in Dallas. She and her husband now divide their time between homes in Texas and South Carolina.

Can't wait for the next sizzling novel
by Sandra Brown?

Get ready to turn up the heat with

Temperatures

Rising

by

Sandra Brown

On sale now

Read on for a sneak peek at this

breathtaking scorcher

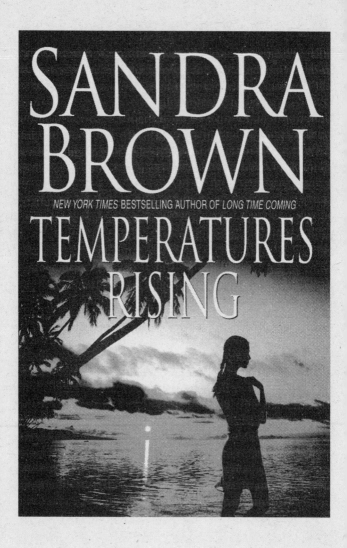

SANDRA
BROWN

NEW YORK TIMES BESTSELLING AUTHOR OF *LONG TIME COMING*

TEMPERATURES
RISING

Temperatures Rising
On sale now

One

Sloe-eyed. Sleek hair. Slender figure.

Scout Ritland mentally summed up his first impressions of the woman he spotted across the ballroom. She was a stunner, a definite standout.

Between the two of them milled a crowd of black-tie-clad celebrants getting drunk on self-congratulations and a tropical fruit punch that made even the stuffiest imbiber feel loose enough to skip naked through the Pacific surf.

Scout wasn't quite that far gone, but he was experiencing a pleasant buzz. It was as loud as the calls of the night birds in the jungle surrounding the landscaped grounds of the Coral Reef, the spectacular resort that was enjoying its official grand opening tonight.

The potent punch had a tendency to thaw inhibitions, suppress morals, and vanquish previously held ideals pertaining to sexual equality. Eyes glazed by intemperance and uncharacteristic chauvinism, Scout stared at the woman in the clinging white dress. Without a smidgen of remorse he was assessing her only as a sex object.

Parrish Island had that effect on people. The place, no more than a dot in a chain of dots on a map of the South Pacific, was intoxicating. Fragrant flowers, banyan trees, and coconut palms abounded; Yankee pomposity did not.

Only a few hours earlier Scout had finally succumbed to the island's allure. For the first time since his arrival months before, he had looked beyond the shell-pink-marble walls of the hotel. Up till now it had consumed so much of his time, energy, and thought, he hadn't had an opportunity to enjoy the unspoiled island and its friendly inhabitants.

One inhabitant in particular—the woman in white. Damn, she was gorgeous. Aloof. Even a trifle haughty. She had noticed his stare and had returned it with a cool appraisal of her own. Then, as though nothing about him could possibly interest her, she had studiously ignored him ever since.

Scout was intrigued. He hadn't seen her around the resort while it was still under construction, so she wasn't a hotel employee. The wife of an employee?

That was a hell of a dismal thought. He discarded it along with his recently emptied glass. If she was married, where was her husband? What guy in his right mind would let a woman who looked like her run around loose in a room full of men who had been separated from hearth and home for months?

No, Scout doubted she was married or seriously attached. She didn't have a "taken" look about her. Then who was she, he wondered as he disinterestedly surveyed the array of exotic foods on one of the buffet tables while keeping her in sight.

"Great job, Mr. Ritland," someone commented in passing.

"Thanks."

A large portion of the resort hotel was built out over the waters of a placid lagoon. Scout had engineered the marvel, working together with the architect. Because of his ingenious efforts, he was receiving his share of the glory. His hand had been shaken so many times, it was cramping. His shoulder was sore where it had been heartily slapped in congratulations for a job well done.

Reeling with the inebriation more of success than of the fruit punch, he wended his way through the crowd. His destination was the woman standing beneath one of the high, arched openings leading outside.

When he got within speaking distance, she turned suddenly and looked directly at him. Scout was stopped dead in his tracks. He sucked in a quick breath.

The almond-shaped eyes, tilted up slightly at the corners, weren't dark brown as he had expected, but blue. Neon blue. Electrifying and stupefying blue.

"Scout, where are you off to? Glad I caught you before you got away."

His elbow was grabbed from behind and he was brought around. Keeping his gaze locked with the woman's for as long as possible, his head reluctantly followed his body around. "Ah, Mr. Reynolds." He shook the hand extended to him.

"Corey," the hotel magnate corrected Scout. "You've done a terrific job. Getting tired of hearing that yet?"

Scout shook his head and laughed self-derisively. "Never."

"It goes without saying how pleased we are. I speak for everyone in the corporation."

"Thank you, sir." Scout couldn't afford to be rude to the man who had signed his hefty paychecks, but he glanced quickly over his shoulder. She had disappeared. Damn!

"It wasn't an easy undertaking," Corey Reynolds was

saying. "Especially when one considers all the hardship you faced during the construction."

Scout asked, "You mean the islanders' attitude toward work?" The other man nodded. "They definitely do no comprehend the meaning of deadlines or the eight-hou workday," Scout said ruefully. "Overtime incentives neve lured them away from a celebration, and they have abou ten of those a month. That didn't bother me nearly as mucl as the thievery, though. I apologize again for going ove budget on the supplies."

"It wasn't your fault that they kept disappearing. know you tried every way you could think of to catch the thieves."

"Wily bastards," Scout said beneath his breath. " even sat up four nights straight keeping vigil. The night decided that it was futile and went to bed, we were hi again."

Catching a glimpse of white out of the corner of hi eye, Scout swiveled his head toward the terrace. There wa nothing there but moonlight and sultry, fragrant air. Was sh still out there, lurking in the shadows of the tropical gardens

". . . with yourself?"

"Huh?" What had Mr. Reynolds asked him? Oh, yes "No, I haven't seen anything of the island except the are immediately around here. I thought I'd take off a week or s before flying home."

"Good idea. Give yourself time to wind down befor your wedding. I presume it's still on."

"Late next month."

Mr. Reynolds smiled and asked, "How is Mis Colfax?"

Corey Reynolds had been introduced to Jennife Colfax at a dinner party in Boston, where Reynolds Grou was headquartered. At that point the Coral Reef resort ha been only an architectural rendering. It pleased Scout that the CEO remembered his fiancée's name. He could always count on Jennifer to make a good impression.

"Her letters indicate that she's fine," he replied.

"Still beautiful?"

Scout grinned expansively. "Very."

The older man chuckled. "You're a trusting young man to leave her for this long a time."

"We came to an understanding before I left. I couldn't very well expect her to sit home alone every night while I was away. She's been free to date, as long as it's kept on a platonic basis."

"You're not only trustful, but generous. Still, I know she's eager to have her fiancé back in the States."

Scout shrugged. "She went to Europe for several weeks during the summer. And she's had her aunt's antiques shop to help keep her busy."

"Oh?" Reynolds inquired with polite interest. "What does she do there?"

"*Dabbles* is the word that comes to mind." Jennifer did a lot of dabbling—in antiques, in music, in fashion.

"My wife dabbles too. When she's not shopping," Corey Reynolds added on a laugh. Sipping at his glass of punch, he asked, "Lovely, aren't they?"

Scout followed the direction of Mr. Reynolds's gaze. He was watching one of the island girls hired for the night to serve canapés. She was dressed in a short floral-print sarong that had been artfully wrapped around her lithe body. Like most of the island women, she was petite and very pretty, with glossy black hair, snapping dark eyes, and a ready smile.

"Even though I'm engaged to be married," Scout said, "I haven't failed to notice that one of Parrish Island's natural resources is its lovely female population."

Reynolds directed his attention back to Scout. "What do you plan to do here on the island during your R and R?"

"Lose myself. Escape from delays, slow-moving workers, and the telephone. Go fishing. Maybe get in some hunting. Body-surf. Lie on the beach and do absolutely nothing." He leaned forward and added, "If I get captured by a lovely, bare-breasted native girl, don't come looking for me anytime soon."

Corey Reynolds chuckled and slapped him on the back. "You rascal. I like your sense of humor." They shook hands and, again, Corey Reynolds praised Scout's engineering feat. "I'll see you back in Boston. I want to talk over some future projects with you. Let's you, the lovely Jennifer, and I have lunch soon."

"We would enjoy that very much, sir. Thank you."

Watching the older man move away, Scout was barely able to contain his excitement. He didn't want to become part of the Reynolds Group. His personality didn't fit the corporate mode. He would find that environment creatively stifling. But he certainly wanted another contract with the Group, and it looked as though that was what Corey Reynolds had in mind.

The Coral Reef resort project had been Scout's first break into the big time. He knew the importance of capitalizing on his success while he was still on the minds of the decision makers.

After his talk with Corey Reynolds, he felt even more that he had something to celebrate. Taking another glass of punch from a waitress bearing a silver tray, he moved through the archway to the terrace beyond.

The exterior walls of the sprawling resort were garnished with bougainvillea vines heavy with clusters of their vibrant flowers. No expense had been spared to decorate the hotel inside and out. Priceless Oriental urns held lush ferns and ornamental palms. Natural plumeria trees had been pruned to perfection. Like gigantic fireflies, torches flickered inside stonework lanterns, strategically placed along winding paths through the gardens.

From the main terrace, wide, shallow steps led down to another level. One path curved left toward the trilevel swimming pool with its manmade waterfall and ornate fountains. Another path led down to the beach, where the sand was a pale blond ribbon between the manicured lawn and the gently lapping surf.

Revelers seeking privacy had drifted out of the ballroom. A group of Asian men discussed business over drinks at a table on the lower terrace. Beneath a palm tree on the lawn a couple kissed, oblivious to everything except each other. Another couple strolled hand-in-hand in the surf, still wearing their evening clothes, their shoes dangling from their hands.

In the center of the moonlit panorama stood a solitary figure. Scout, as one under the command of a hypnotist, moved down the steps toward her. The moonlight on her white dress made her as visible in the darkness as the beacon of a lighthouse. She stood motionless, facing the ocean, staring across the water as though communing with it in a silent and sacred manner.

Helluva dress, Scout thought as he moved closer. Jennifer wouldn't have approved of it. Not many New England women would have. It was painfully simple but blatantly sexy. There was a high slit on one thigh. One shoulder was left completely bare by the form-fitting garment. The balmy breeze molded its fabric to her, delineating her breasts and the V of her thighs.

Scout's thoughts were the same ones that kept priests in business.

He felt a momentary stab of guilt because of Jennifer.

But she was on the other side of the world. This island seemed as far removed from Jennifer and Boston as another planet. Rules and codes of behavior that applied there were of no more use here than a woolen overcoat.

He'd been working nonstop for months. He'd earned one night of pleasure, hadn't he? He had been living in one of the most exotic spots on earth and hadn't had a single chance to sample its pleasures.

The rationalizations marched in file through his brain, but even without them he would have acted. Months of sexual abstinence, the potent liquor he'd drunk, the tropical setting, the beautiful woman, were a powerful combination of aphrodisiacs he couldn't resist.

Hearing his approach, she turned her head and gave him another piercing stare with those breathtaking blue eyes. Hair darker than midnight had been pulled back into a low bun on her nape and decorated with two white hibiscus blossoms. Her only jewelry was a pair of single pearl earrings, each pearl as large as a marble.

As flawless as they were, their opalescence was no competition for her skin. It was creamy, smooth, incredibly flawless. There was a lot of it showing too. Neck. Chest. The curve of one breast. Legs. She wasn't wearing stockings with the high-heel sandals. Even her feet were pretty. So were her hands. In one she carried a small satin evening bag.

Such loveliness, such rarity, such perfection. Scout's body was pulsing with lust.

She was standing beside a piece of sculpture. It represented a pagan god who was wearing a puckish grin and sporting an exaggerated phallus. Scout remembered the day they'd set the statue in place. It had been the talk of the work site. There'd been a round of jokes made, each more lewd than the preceding one.

Now he could swear the statue's insolent grin was aimed at him. It was as if the little devil knew about his physical condition and was maliciously delighted. He nodded at the idol and spoke to the woman.

"Friend of yours?"

He was hoping for the best, but halfway expected her to rebuff him. His heart expanded when her lips, glossy and tinted, parted in a smile that revealed teeth as flawless as everything else.

"He's everybody's friend. He's a god of eroticism."

Ah, good. Language wouldn't be a barrier. She spoke English. It was accented, but beautifully so. Her voice was low and husky, with the whisper of the surf behind it.

Scout smiled wryly. "I could have guessed that. What's his name?"

She told him. He frowned. "That has at least twelve syllables and they're all vowels." Since his arrival, he'd mastered a few words of the native dialect, but they all had to do with construction. "Get back to work" was hardly what he wanted to say to this woman.

But even if he'd known the correct words, he couldn't say what was on his mind. *This little guy has nothing on me in the arousal department. I'm hard as a rock, and, baby, you're the reason. Your place or mine?* Those words hardly seemed appropriate for opening a conversation.

"My name's Scout Ritland." He extended his hand.

She gave him hers. It was cool and small and soft. "Chantal duPont." Withdrawing her hand, she added, "It was a pleasure to meet you, Mr. Ritland," and turned to go.

It took a moment for Scout to recover from her dazzling smile and the feel of her hand in his. When he did, he fell into step alongside her as she took one of the shell-gravel paths toward the perimeter of the resort's property.

"Will you be working at the hotel?" he asked in an effort to prolong their brief conversation.

She shot him an amused glance. "Hardly, Mr. Ritland."

"Then what were you doing at the party?"

"I was invited."

He was forced to catch her arm in order to detain her. She came around to face him. The moon cast intriguing shadows over her face through the overhead trees. "I didn't mean to sound rude," he explained. "Of course you were invited. It's just that I haven't seen you around, and I wondered what—"

"I didn't take offense," she interrupted softly.

He stared down at her, captivated by her exquisite face, her eyes, her mouth. His fingers were still around her upper arm. He'd never felt softer skin. Her eyes moved down and pointedly called attention to the fact that he was still touching her.

Regrettably, he relaxed his hold. Only when he dropped that hand to his side did he realize that in his other, he was still carrying the glass of punch.

"Care for a drink?" he asked, feeling a little ridiculous.

"No, thank you."

"Can't say that I blame you. It's stronger than a swift kick from a mule."

Giving him a ghost of a smile, she reached for the glass and brought it to her lips. Watching him over the rim, she drained it, then ran her tongue over her lips, licking up every drop. "Unless you've cultivated a tolerance for it, Mr. Ritland." She passed him the empty glass and stepped off the path, entering the jungle.

Scout stared after her, amazed. That much liquor, imbibed that quickly, would have knocked most grown men flat on their backs. She'd swallowed it like mother's milk and was still standing. Not only that, she was negotiating the dark jungle path as silently and expertly as a nocturnal predator. Leaves barely stirred with her passage. No sooner had he formed that thought than she slipped through a screen of vines and disappeared.

He dropped the glass on the overgrown path and charged after her, thrashing his way through dense foliage, mindless of his tuxedo. An insect whizzed past his ear like a missile; he swatted at it heedlessly.

"Chantal?"

"*Oui?*"

He spun around. She was standing almost even with him, as though having materialized from one of the trees. Feeling like a complete fool now, he clumsily untied his bow tie. "What are you, a nymph or something?"

She laughed, a breathy, stirring sound. "I'm quite human, flesh and blood, just like you."

He loosed the collar button of his pleated shirt, but then his fingers fell still. Again he was arrested by her remarkable uniqueness. His eyes started at the top of her sleek head and moved over her face, along her graceful neck, across her full breasts, and down the center of her enticing body.

"Human, yes. Flesh and blood, definitely." He took enough steps to bring him toe to toe with her. "But just like me? No. Hell no. You're like nobody I've ever seen before."

He had to touch her again to reassure himself that she was real. He touched the curve of her breast first, that smooth expanse swelling above the neckline of her dress almost even with the notch of her shoulder. It was as marvelous to touch as it was to look at. He rubbed it lightly with the knuckle of his index finger.

Then he slid his fingertip up and down her neck and

followed it up to her exquisitely chiseled jawbone. When his hand curved around the nape of her neck, she relaxed it and let her head bend back slightly, offering her lips up to the first soft brushing caress of his.

The fruity alcohol was sweet on her breath. Its essence filled his head, aroused his body, inflamed his passions. His tongue flicked along her lips. He groaned her name, a name as enchanting as she.

In response, she placed her hand inside his jacket and laid it on the muscled wall of his chest. His lips parted above hers, pressed, then kissed her in earnest as his other arm closed around her waist.

She was as pliant as damp sand, conforming her body to fit the shape of his. Scout felt the firm thrust of her breasts, the delectable softness of her femininity, the suppleness of her thighs. His skull exploded with desire. He moved one hand to her breast and caressed it through her dress. Beneath the soft cloth he felt her nipple harden against the circular motions of his thumb.

His tongue entered her mouth hungrily. Time and again he sampled her taste, withdrawing his tongue to savor the delicacy of her lips, dipping again into the dark, sweet recess of her mouth.

His heart hammered painfully in his chest. His sex, heavy and thick, throbbed with each heartbeat. He nestled it in her cleft. His hand cupped her derriere and tilted her up and forward against him, wondering what she would think of his full hardness and hoping that she would respond favorably.

He moaned with gratification when he felt her hand fumbling between their bodies at waist level, obviously in search of his zipper tab.

That's why he was stunned to feel something hard and cold being shoved into his midriff. No sooner had that startling realization registered than she pulled free of him and stepped out of reach.

"What the hell is—"

The question froze on his lips when he lowered his gaze to the pistol, the barrel of which was aimed straight at his belly button.

Scout gaped at her. "What the hell are you doing?"

"I'm pointing a pistol at you, Mr. Ritland," she stated calmly in her accented English. "And unless you do everything I say, I'm prepared to shoot you."

Her expression was deadly serious, but Scout found it difficult to take her threat at face value. There were plenty of adjectives to describe her, but menacing wasn't among them.

"Shoot me? For what?" he asked, guffawing. "For kissing you?"

"For wrongly presuming that I wanted to be kissed and pawed like a waterfront prostitute."

He propped his hands on his hips. "What was I supposed to think after you lured me out here?"

"I didn't *lure* you."

"The hell you didn't," he said, his temper flaring.

"You followed me. I didn't encourage you."

His amusement had vanished. "Don't pull that self-righteous crap on me, princess. You wanted me to follow you. Your rejection was your come-on. You liked the kiss and everything else," he said with a sly glance down at her breasts and their projecting centers. "You can't very well pretend you didn't when I can plainly see otherwise."

Her eyes went dangerously bright as she pulled herself up to military erectness. "This isn't about your kisses."

"Then what?"

"You'll find out soon enough. Turn around and start walking."

He snorted another laugh as he peered into the impenetrable foliage surrounding them. "Forgive the cliché, but it's a jungle out there."

"Walk, Mr. Ritland."

"Like hell."

"Need I remind you that I've got you at gunpoint and you'd be wise to do as I say?"

His lips curled into an arrogant smirk. "Oh, I'm real scared," he whispered tauntingly. "A woman who looks like a goddess and kisses like an expensive whore is dangerous, all right. But her weapon of choice is not a handgun."

Outraged, she cried, "How dare you—"

He lunged for the pistol. They wrestled for control of it.

Chantal gave a small, surprised exclamation as the gun went off in her hand. They stood frozen, staring at each other with incredulity. Then Scout staggered back a step and looked down at his thigh. It was pumping blood.

"You shot me," he said, stupidly stating the obvious. Then, angrily, "You shot me! You actually shot me!"

The delayed pain finally slammed into him. It had the impetus of a major leaguer's pitch finding the center of the catcher's mitt. Lights exploded around him. He gaped at his wound, gaped at the woman, then issued the roar of an enraged beast and lunged for her again.

This time the pain came crashing down on the base of his skull. He collapsed onto the spongy jungle floor. Overhead, through the trees, he saw colored lights flashing and popping like an electric kaleidoscope.

Then the night edged in and blotted out everything.